She pulled onto ~~the driveway and parked.~~ **Only then did she notice the man seated on her front steps.**

Jon Redmond waited until she climbed out of the vehicle before he rose to greet her.

Her pulse accelerated as she mentally braced herself and moved onto the brick walkway. She gave him a quick once-over, taking in the dark circles under his eyes and the lines of exhaustion that had deepened around his mouth. She could have sworn he had on the same clothes he'd worn to the crime scene at two o'clock in the morning, only now they were far from crisp, and he didn't seem at all pulled together. The opposite, in fact. The day had obviously taken a toll.

She said, not unkindly, "You look like death warmed over and I would know."

THE SECRETS
SHE HID

AMANDA STEVENS

 Harlequin

INTRIGUE

Harlequin® INTRIGUE™

ISBN-13: 978-1-335-45743-1

The Secrets She Hid

Harlequin Enterprises ULC
22 Adelaide St. West, 41st Floor
Toronto, Ontario M5H 4E3, Canada
www.Harlequin.com

Printed in Lithuania

MIX
Paper | Supporting responsible forestry
FSC® C021394

Amanda Stevens is an award-winning author of over fifty novels, including the modern gothic series The Graveyard Queen. Her books have been described as eerie and atmospheric and "a new take on the classic ghost story." Born and raised in the rural South, she now resides in Houston, Texas, where she enjoys binge-watching, bike riding and the occasional margarita.

Books by Amanda Stevens

Harlequin Intrigue

Pine Lake

Whispering Springs

Digging Deeper

The Secret of Shutter Lake

The Killer Next Door

The Secrets She Hid

A Procedural Crime Story

Little Girl Gone
John Doe Cold Case
Looks That Kill

An Echo Lake Novel

Without a Trace
A Desperate Search
Someone Is Watching

Visit the Author Profile page at Harlequin.com.

CAST OF CHARACTERS

Veda Campion—The forensic pathologist is recruited by an old antagonist to help solve the murder of the man who killed her sister seventeen years ago.

Jon Redmond—Now a DA in rural Mississippi, he's devoted his whole adult life to proving his brother's innocence. When Tony Redmond is murdered, Jon turns to the one woman with reason to despise him.

Tony Redmond—A former high school football star convicted of brutally murdering his childhood sweetheart.

Chief Marcus Campion—Did the police chief, along with the former DA and the current coroner, dispose of evidence that could have cleared Tony Redmond?

Owen Campion—He attacked Tony Redmond and vowed to kill him just days before Tony turned up dead.

Michael Legend—The older married mystery lover had a lot to lose if his affair with Lily Campion came to light.

Clay Stipes—An ex-con and former cellmate of Tony's claims he has information that could lead Jon Redmond to the real killer. Just how far is he willing to go to collect a payday?

Chapter One

The ringtone pealed persistently. With a muttered oath, Veda Campion snaked an arm from beneath the covers to grope for the phone on the nightstand. Shoving aside the quilt, she glanced at the screen. Her brother's name shocked her awake, and she sprang up in bed.

"Nate? What's wrong? Has something happened to Mom?"

His voice boomed back reassuringly. "Relax. She's fine as far as I know. I had dinner with her early last evening."

"Thank God." They were all still on edge since their mother's heart attack six months ago. Veda leaned back against the headboard and swiped tangles from her face as she frowned into the darkness. "Then, why are you calling at two in morning?"

"Did you forget you're the acting coroner until Dr. Bader gets back from vacation?"

"No, of course I didn't forget. I'm still half-asleep, is all." Actually, her temporary position really had slipped her mind. She blamed the memory lapse on exhaustion and a lingering irritation that she'd been so easily manipulated by her former mentor. Dr. Bader had been persistent about his future plans for her despite her objections to the contrary. She had no interest in returning to her hometown on a permanent basis. Yet somehow her unpaid leave from the Orleans Parish Coroner's Office had turned into a resignation, and the next thing she knew she'd signed a short-term lease on a furnished bungalow in Milton, Mississippi, while she contemplated her next career move.

"Veda? You still with me?"

The question dragged her back into the conversation. "Yes, I'm here. What's going on?"

"A body was found in Cedarville Cemetery earlier tonight. A group of partying teenagers called it in." His tone subtly shifted as tension hardened his delivery. He was no longer her older brother but instead a seasoned police detective following protocol. "We can't finish processing the scene until you come out here and take charge of the body."

She swung her legs over the side of the bed, adrenaline already starting to pump. "You've kept the area clean?"

"Relatively speaking. The first responders set up a perimeter and established an entry point, and we've limited the number of personnel we're letting through the gates. Even so, forensics is going to be a bear on this one. Those kids left footprints all over the damn place. The more time goes by, the greater the chance for contamination."

"Did they touch the body?"

"They swear they didn't, but those footprints tell a different story. I wouldn't be surprised if they texted close-ups of the victim to some of their friends. We'll be damn lucky if the images don't turn up on social media."

Veda nodded absently as she rose. With the phone pressed to her ear, she strode across the room and started pulling clothes from her closet with one hand. "You think it's a homicide?"

"Officially, that's for you to determine, but we've got a male Caucasian shot in the back of the head. So yeah, I'd say we're definitely dealing with a homicide." Nate lowered his voice as if wary of being overheard. "Brace yourself. The victim is Tony Redmond."

Veda froze, one hand still grasping the phone, the other a clean pair of jeans. She let the jeans fall to the floor. "Are you sure?"

"Pretty damn sure, even though he's lying facedown in the dirt."

She closed her eyes and said on a breath, "My God, Nate."

"I know. I wasn't expecting to start my week like this."

"Start your week?"

"Check the calendar. It's officially Monday morning."

"You say he was found prone?" Veda took a moment to collect her composure before asking the obvious questions. "*You* didn't touch him, did you? You didn't roll him over?"

"Didn't have to. I recognized his tattoos."

She went back over to the bed and sat down on the edge as she tried to wrap her head around the news. Her sister's killer shot dead in the same cemetery where Lily had been laid to rest seventeen years ago. Veda didn't know how to react. She had an odd sense of relief—a lightness—that left her feeling ashamed. They were talking about a human being, after all. A son, a brother.

Then dread descended. Justice might have been served, but by whom?

Her heart started to pound, and her mouth went suddenly dry. She swallowed and tried to calm her racing pulse. "You haven't been alone with the body, have you, Nate?"

He sounded annoyed. "Do you even need to ask that question? Give me some credit."

"I know. I know. I just don't want anything coming back on you. On any of us. This is tricky, given our history with Tony Redmond."

"You don't need to worry about me. The officers who responded to the call were still on the scene when I arrived. As soon as I recognized the victim, I alerted the chief. He's already assigned another detective to take lead."

She noted his use of their uncle's title rather than his first name. Probably her brother's way of trying to subvert any notion of favoritism within the police department. He wouldn't like having his credentials called into question. "That's for the best, I suppose, though I doubt the gesture will appease the Redmonds. Conflict of interest in this town goes all the way to the top. None of us should be anywhere near this case. You, me or Marcus."

"It is what it is," Nate said. "We're small-town law enforcement. Our resources and manpower are limited. We don't have the luxury of picking and choosing our cases. You're the only coroner we've got until Dr. Bader returns from his trip."

"He'll be back first thing in the morning. *This* morning. You couldn't have waited a few hours?" she added with a note of sarcasm.

"You'll have to talk to the killer about his timing. If it's any consolation, I did try Dr. Bader's number. He's not picking up."

Veda took another breath, still with that anvil of dread hanging over her head. Her hand slipped to her throat as unwelcome images streamed from a dark corner of her subconscious. She didn't want to think such thoughts, but she couldn't seem to shut off the spigot. "Has his family been notified?"

"Not yet. We're waiting for the official death pronouncement."

She turned on the bed so that she could stare out the window. She had a sudden notion of red eyes watching her from the darkness. Nothing but fantasy, of course. There were no demons in downtown Milton, Mississippi. Only murderers.

"What a sad and sordid ending to Tony Redmond's story," she murmured. "He's been out of prison for only a few weeks, and now this. In spite of everything, I can't help feeling sorry for his mother. She finally got her son back only to lose him for good this time. I can only imagine how hard his death will hit her."

"You and I don't have to imagine, do we?" Rather than an angry comeback, Nate's response seemed measured. "We saw what Lily's murder did to our own mother. She'll never get over it. None of us will."

Veda frowned at his tone. He sounded calm, yet she knew his emotions had to be in turmoil like hers. Lily's killer dead after all these years. Shot in the back of the head by an as-yet unknown assailant. Was it justice or revenge? Or completely unrelated to their sister's murder, as Veda fervently hoped? For some reason, Nate's low-key delivery only deepened her unease.

"Are you okay?" she asked.

"Why wouldn't I be?"

She was reluctant to explain her concern. "You're saying all the right things, but you sound…odd. Almost too cool under the circumstances."

She could imagine his shrug on the other end. "What do you expect? I've been doing this job for a long time. I know how to handle myself. I'm not about to let my emotions or personal animus toward the victim and his family get in the way of doing what has to be done. I'm better than that."

"I know you are."

"But between us? Between you and me?" He paused for a long moment as if debating on how much he would allow to slip through the cracks. "I won't be losing any sleep over what happened out here tonight. As far as I'm concerned, Tony Redmond got what was coming to him."

"You probably shouldn't say that, even to me," she cautioned. "The Redmonds will be looking for any excuse to point fingers."

"I said what we're both thinking. As for his family, they moved heaven and earth to get that creep out of prison. Jon Redmond became an attorney for the sole purpose of working on his brother's appeal. Then he had the nerve to come back here and run for DA so that he could make sure the charges wouldn't be refiled once he got Tony released. He played the long game, and it backfired on him tonight. I bet he'll wish in hindsight he'd left well enough alone. If Tony had been behind bars where he belonged, he'd still be alive."

"That's harsh, Nate."

"It's the truth. Isn't that what you wanted to hear?"

"Maybe, but let's be honest. Would either of us have done any different in Jon Redmond's shoes?"

"Luckily, we don't need to wonder because our brother didn't kill anyone."

Veda found herself shivering despite the summer heat. She tried to ignore the suffocating chill, but an ugly premonition had been slithering closer and closer from the moment she'd answered Nate's call.

She fell silent, loath to give credence to the terrible

thoughts running through her head. But she needed to be candid with Nate so that he could dispel her doubts. "Speaking of our brother, when was the last time you spoke with Owen?"

Nate's voice sharpened. "Why?"

"When did you last see him?" she pressed.

"Don't go there," he warned.

She tightened her grip on the phone. "I don't want to, but how can I not after everything that's happened?"

"Damn it, Veda Louise."

"Don't *Veda Louise* me. Whether you want to admit it or not, Owen could be in big trouble."

"For what? It was a scuffle. Stop trying to make a mountain out of a molehill."

"Trust me, I'm not. You've only heard Owen's version of the fight, and he downplayed what happened for Mom's sake. But I was there, and I'm telling you it was vicious. You should have seen the way he and Tony went after each other. I thought one of them would end up dead on the street, and there wasn't a damn thing I could do to stop them. It took four grown men to pull them apart."

"What's your point, Veda?"

"I'm not the only one who saw Owen throw the first punch. Even after it was over, he couldn't keep his mouth shut. He told Tony Redmond if he ever came near anyone in his family again, he'd kill him."

Nate swore.

"You see why I'm worried? I don't want to say it. I don't want to even think it—"

"Then, don't," Nate said. "Owen is home in bed asleep."

"You know that for a fact?"

"I've no reason to believe otherwise, and neither do you."

"We can't just wish this away, Nate. Too many people saw and heard what Owen did. Once those witnesses come forward, our little brother could find himself at the top of the suspect list."

She heard Nate draw a breath. "I'll be the first to admit Owen's behavior does him no favors. He's always been a hothead. I've wanted to throttle him myself more times than I can count. But he's not a killer. Remember that before you go borrowing trouble. For now, focus on your job, and let the police worry about suspects."

If only she could let it go that easily. The public confrontation—undoubtedly captured by at least one cell phone—was enough to trigger suspicion. Unless Owen had an airtight alibi for the time of death, no one would be able to protect him. Not Nate. Not their uncle. Certainly not Veda. She prayed he was home in bed asleep, but even then, unless he had a companion, he'd have no way of verifying his whereabouts.

Earlier, she'd been sympathetic about how the news would affect Theresa Redmond, but what about her own mother? The investigation would take a toll on both families, just as it had seventeen years ago. She could still hear the dread in her mother's voice when she learned of Owen's clash with Tony Redmond.

Promise me you won't go near that man again. I'm serious, Owen. If he decides to press charges, you could end up in jail. I couldn't take that. You behind bars, and Lily's killer free to do as he pleases. I couldn't bear to lose another child.

I'm not going to jail, and you're not going to lose me. You're not going to lose any of us. Right, Nate? Right, Veda? We have each other's backs no matter what.

No matter what.

"Veda?"

"Still here."

"How soon can you get to the scene?"

She shook off the memory and stood. "Fifteen minutes. Front or back entrance?"

"Front. You'll see the lights. And Veda?"

"What?"

"Just do what has to be done tonight and then back off. Dr. Bader will be back on the job in a few hours. Let him handle the postmortem. No reason for you to be involved beyond the death pronouncement."

Just do what has to be done tonight and then back off.

She told herself not to dwell on the implication as she pulled on jeans and a plain white T-shirt. No reason to speculate as to why her big brother seemed so eager to isolate her from the investigation. Not yet, at least.

JON REDMOND YAWNED as he glanced at the time on his phone. It was just after two in the morning and he'd yet to close his eyes. He was too wired to sleep. Too anxious about what his brother might be up to tonight. Instead of going to bed, he'd been sitting on the balcony of his second-story apartment for the past three hours willing his phone to ring. He told himself for the umpteenth time that he was over-reacting. Letting his imagination get the better of him. Tony had only been incommunicado for a few hours. No need to anticipate the worst. But coming on the heels of their recent blowout, his brother's silence worried Jon. A lot.

Sipping the bourbon he'd been nursing for hours, he went back over everything that had happened earlier in the evening in case he'd missed a clue. He'd left the office around nine and swung by their mother's place hoping to find Tony in the small guesthouse where he'd been staying since his release from prison. The two brothers had unfinished business to discuss, and Jon had been determined to keep his cool this time. No easy feat, considering everything that had gone down between them during their last confrontation.

Ever since an ex-con named Clay Stipes had hit town, the whole family had been on edge. Stipes posed a myriad of potential problems for Tony and now for Jon. In hindsight, his career as the Webber County DA—not to mention his peace of mind—might have been better served by remaining in the dark, but too late for that now. He'd demanded the truth, and now he found himself embroiled in a mess that could have far-reaching consequences. The sooner he and Tony hashed out a plan to deal with Clay Stipes, the sooner they could send him on his way and put his threats behind them.

But the windows in the guesthouse had been dark, and the front door locked. Jon's knock had gone unanswered as had his text messages and voice mails. He'd left the property without stopping by to see his mother. He didn't want to worry her or his younger sister Gabby unless it became absolutely necessary to bring them into the loop. Having Tony home from prison after seventeen years was a big enough adjustment. No need to exacerbate an already stressful situation.

Instead, Jon had driven around town for a couple of hours checking the parking lots of local bars and watering holes. He'd gone inside a few of the places he knew Tony had recently frequented to see if anyone remembered seeing him that night, either alone or with a companion. No such luck.

Finally, he'd given up the search and gone home. Tony

was a grown man. He'd survived nearly two decades in a maximum-security prison. Jon reminded himself that if anyone knew how to take care of himself, it was his brother.

Yet here he sat drinking and brooding when there wasn't a damn thing he could do about the situation until the bank opened at nine. He already had an appointment. All he had to do was go in and apply for a loan. He and the bank manager had gone to high school together. They'd played on the same baseball team. That should count for something. He had good credit, a decent salary and a small piece of land that could be used for collateral. He should be able to get his hands on a significant amount of money without too much effort. Once the funds were transferred into his account, he and Tony could figure out their next move.

He finished the remainder of his drink in one quick gulp. The burn of the alcohol did little to alleviate his unease. Another drink might have helped, but he resisted the temptation. *Stay calm, keep a clear head.* Clay Stipes was a dangerous man. Not just an ex-con but a former cop who'd killed his partner. That he'd gotten out after serving ten years was a testament to the weaknesses and loopholes in the judicial system. But then, he supposed there were those who thought the same about Tony's release.

Bottom line, neither brother could afford to let down his guard until Stipes agreed to leave town. Maybe not even then. Trusting a blackmailer to keep his word was asking for trouble, but Jon didn't see any other way out. Stipes had the upper hand. As long as Marcus Campion remained chief of police, going to the cops wasn't an option.

As the minutes continued to tick by, he grew more and more restless. He reconsidered calling his mother, but she would be fast asleep at this hour, and a phone call would only panic her. He could text Gabby instead. College had turned his little sister into a night owl. He had a feeling she'd still be up, and she had a view of the backyard from her bedroom window. He could at least ask her to check to see if the lights were on in the guesthouse or if Tony's truck was in the driveway. Still, he hesitated. Once he sounded the alarm, there would be no going back.

Then go to bed. What the hell do you hope to accomplish by sitting out here all night?

He got up, but instead of going inside, he moved to the balcony railing and peered down into the manicured grounds of his apartment complex. He was so tense that for a moment he imagined Clay Stipes in the park across the street staring up at his apartment. In the next instant, he realized the sinister shadow was a bush. Not a good sign when he started conjuring bad guys from shrubbery.

Not a good sign and not at all like him. During the seventeen years of his brother's incarceration, he'd managed to keep a level head even in the darkest of times. Compartmentalization was the key. He'd learned how to shut down his racing thoughts the moment his head hit the pillow. It was the only way he'd been able to survive all those years of burning the candle at both ends. He supposed it was ironic and more than a little unsettling that he hadn't had a decent night's sleep since his brother's release.

There'd been a moment, however, as he'd watched his brother walk through the prison gates a free man when the weight of the world seemed to lift from his shoulders. Everything he'd worked so hard for his entire adult life had come to fruition, and his family finally had a chance to heal and be whole again.

The elation had faded almost at once because his brother's

physical appearance outside the prison walls was shocking. Looking back, Jon wasn't sure why he'd reacted so viscerally. After all, he'd witnessed firsthand Tony's transformation over the years. The wavy hair that had once made high-school girls swoon had grown down his back, and he wore it pulled back in a scraggly, dull ponytail. Then came the crazy patchwork of tattoos all up and down his arms and around his neck. The boyish swagger of a high-school football star was replaced by the surly wariness of a convict. He'd bulked up because prison was about nothing if not survival of the fittest.

During his first few days of freedom, Tony had spent most of his time sitting in the sun with his face tipped to the sky. By the end of the second week, he'd begun to open up a little about his time in prison and to even crack a smile now and then. He started to talk about getting a job and maybe going back to school. His plans for the future thrilled their mother. Jon hadn't seen her so happy in years. Everything seemed to be working out until Clay Stipes blew into town with a murder-for-hire scheme that threatened to ensnare the whole Redmond family.

The peal of the ringtone startled him from a deep reverie. He picked up the phone and answered anxiously. "Tony? Where the hell have you been all night?"

The caller hesitated before identifying himself. "This is Marcus Campion." Another pause. "I'm afraid I have some bad news about your brother."

A FEW MINUTES after Nate's call, Veda headed to the garage to check her kit and the supplies she kept in the back of her SUV. A jolt of caffeine would have helped clear the cobwebs, but no time for coffee. She still had a few things to do before she set out for the cemetery. Besides, adrenaline had already made her jittery. Experience had taught her that she was better off sipping water and practicing relaxation techniques on her way to a crime scene.

Her forensic kit included everything from vials and syringes for collecting samples to paper jumpsuits, gloves and shoe covers to protect the crime scene. In a separate bag, she kept rubber boots, sneakers and an extra set of clothing. If the body hadn't yet decomposed, she wouldn't need to change at the scene, but better to be safe than sorry. She'd learned the hard way that the smell of death was nearly impossible to remove from a vehicle once the stench had penetrated the carpet fibers and circulated through the air vents.

She opened the garage door and stepped outside. Drawing in the night air, she stood with eyes closed and tried to ground herself. Images of Lily flitted through her mind. She could almost hear her sister's voice repeating her brother's warning.

Don't borrow trouble, Veda. Be patient and let the answers come to you. You've always been the clever sister. You'll know what to do.

If only that was true, but Veda had never been as shrewd as Lily had made her out to be. She hadn't been blessed with the same powerful combination of beauty and brains that her sister had possessed. Before that fateful night, everyone in town would have sworn Lily Campion had a brilliant future ahead of her. Veda was known as the quiet sister. Smart enough and pretty enough, but never Lily's equal, and she'd always been fine with the comparison. As she grew older, she'd become comfortable in her sister's shadow. With all the attention focused on Lily, Veda could pretty much do as she pleased.

But her sister's murder had changed everything. The once-playful camaraderie between the Campion siblings vanished overnight. Easygoing Nate had morphed into a control freak. Owen, the wild child, became rebellious and reckless. Veda retreated inward. For too many years, they'd remained virtual strangers. Their mother's heart attack had brought them closer, but even now, Veda couldn't say she knew her brothers any more than they knew her. She had no idea what either of them were capable of these days. Tony Redmond's release from prison had pushed a lot of dangerous buttons.

She watched the clouds for a moment longer before climbing into her vehicle and backing down the driveway. Leaving her neighborhood behind, she sped through the deserted streets. As she neared the destination, she began to mentally gear up for the task at hand.

Cedarville Cemetery was located within the city limits, giving the Milton Police Department jurisdiction over the crime scene. The historic graveyard was surrounded on three sides by a forest that cast deep shadows even on the sunniest of days. The place had once fascinated Veda. Some of the interments dated back to the Civil War era, and as a kid, she'd spent many Sunday afternoons with her grandmother wandering through the headstones and monuments.

Like her grandmother, Veda had always sought out quiet little corners, and it could be argued that she still preferred the company of the dead to the living. Not for the first time, she wondered what Lily would think of her profession. Her family had never understood her decision to specialize in forensic pathology, even Nate who knew better than most the value of a skilled medical examiner in the autopsy room.

Her brothers found her professional choices strange and her solitary lifestyle puzzling, and she was okay with that, too.

She pulled her SUV to the curb and parked behind the coroner's van, relieved to note that the movers had already arrived on the scene. She would need one of them to video her examination of the body while the other took photographs. The county morgue was a small office. Everyone pitched in where needed.

The wind was up, and she could see flickers of lightning in the distance. Goose bumps rose at the base of her neck and along her bare arms. She had a bad feeling about the weather.

Climbing into the paper jumpsuit, she grabbed her kit and then followed the voices she heard on the other side of the fence. The sound echoed eerily in the dark, and she found herself shivering again as she approached the gate. Her brother met her just inside. A point of entry had been established using wooden stakes and crime-scene tape. A portable floodlight had been set up near the body, casting a harsh glare over the immediate area. With the backdrop of monuments and mausoleums, the scene struck Veda as surreal.

If she peered beyond the illumination, she could still picture the silhouette of the old stone angel that loomed over the other headstones. She'd once loved the romantic legend behind the crumbling statue, but for a time after Lily's death, Veda could have sworn the angel took on her sister's features. The perceived likeness had unsettled her because rather than emanating a heavenly aura, the marble face seemed icy and judgmental. Rationally, Veda knew the accusatory visage had been born out of her guilt. She wasn't responsible for her sister's murder, and she knew Lily would never have blamed her. Yet how many sleepless nights had she spent agonizing over what she could have said or done to stop her sister from leaving the house that night?

She remained outwardly composed as she tightened her grip on her case.

Nate said quietly at her side, "When was the last time you were here?"

"To Cedarville? Years ago." She glanced around the shadowy landscape. "Hard to believe I used to find this place peaceful. Almost spiritual in a way. Now it just seems sad and oppressive."

"The reason you're here may have something to do with that perception," he said.

"True."

She fell silent, her gaze fixed on the prone outline of her sister's killer. She tried to stay focused, but memories continued to assail her. Lily daydreaming in the backyard hammock. Picking flowers from their mother's garden. In a yellow sundress waving goodbye through the open window of Tony Redmond's truck.

Lily keeping secrets.

Who was he, Lily? The man you fell for that summer. Why wouldn't you tell me his name? And why did he never come forward after you died?

At the back of Veda's mind, a tiny doubt had been flickering for seventeen years. Had the wrong man been sent to prison?

Chapter Two

Veda was jolted back to the present when her uncle came up beside her. He placed his hand lightly on her shoulder. "You made good time getting out here."

She tried to shake off the foreboding that still gripped her as she turned to greet him, but the circumstances and her surroundings made that impossible. "No traffic at this hour. The streets were completely deserted." She suppressed a shiver. "Almost too quiet if you ask me."

"Not for long," he warned. "Only a matter of time before all hell breaks loose."

In his late fifties, Marcus Campion was still lean and rugged with deep lines around his mouth and eyes and a thick head of hair cut military-short. He wasn't in uniform tonight but instead had dressed in jeans, boots and a plaid shirt rolled up to his elbows. His casual attire made him seem more approachable, but his grim expression and ram-rod posture were still intimidating.

"We need to talk about what to expect while we're still out of earshot of the others," he said.

"Can it wait until after I've seen the body?" Veda asked. "The weather could change at any minute."

He cast a quick glance at the sky. "Storm's miles away. Besides, this won't take long, and it's important."

She wanted to remind him that the sooner she did her job, the sooner his people could do theirs, but she intuited from the stubborn set of his mouth and jawline that he intended to say his piece, regardless.

Tamping down her impatience, she nodded.

He kept his voice low as he took a step forward to close the circle. "Once word gets out about Redmond's death, the press will be all over this thing. I wouldn't be surprised if we get national attention, considering what happened seventeen years ago. They'll dredge up every sordid detail of Lily's murder and then some. You need to prepare yourselves for the spectacle. And we all need to try and shield your mother from the worst of it. She's only six months out from her heart attack. The doctors said no stress. The last thing she needs right now is to have her dead daughter's name dragged through the mud again."

"We'll do what we can, of course," Veda said. "But this is the information age. It won't be as simple as turning off the TV."

"She's right," Nate said. "Tony Redmond's murder will be all anyone in this town talks about for months."

Marcus put up a hand and said impatiently, "I don't want to hear any excuses. Just find a way to protect her. After everything she's been through, she deserves a little peace."

Veda wanted to point out that her mother's health was the main reason she'd come back to Milton, but instead she folded her arms and waited.

"Both of you need to keep a low profile until the worst blows over," Marcus said. "That shouldn't be hard. I've assigned the case to Garrett Calloway. He's relatively new in town and doesn't have any connection to either family. He'll pick his own team to work the investigation so your involvement should be minimal, Nate. That goes for you, too, Veda. Dr. Bader will be back in the morgue sometime this morning. Let him handle the postmortem. Keep your distance, and be careful what you say and do in public. Everybody and their dog will be watching. If a reporter corners you, your only comment is *No comment*."

"To that point, should you even be here?" Veda asked. "Wouldn't you and your office be better served if you also kept a low profile? Why not let your lead detective handle the press?"

"Nothing I'd like more," Marcus said. "But I'm the chief of police. I can't palm off my duties and obligations on a subordinate just because I find myself in an uncomfortable position. The public needs to know I'm on the job and that I'll treat this case as I would any other."

"What about Nate?" Veda asked.

Her brother glared at her. "What about me?"

"This isn't your case. There's no reason for you to be here."

"That's not your call."

"Keep it together," Marcus scolded in a hushed voice. He glanced around as a man Veda didn't recognize broke away from a group of cops and approached their huddle. Marcus stepped back to allow the man into their circle. "Veda, this is Detective Garrett Calloway. Garrett, my niece, Veda Campion. She's the acting coroner in Dr. Bader's absence."

Veda extended her hand, and they shook. Calloway looked to be around Nate's age, making him somewhere in his mid- to late thirties. Veda remembered her brother mentioning that the detective had been with the Memphis Police Department before moving back to rural Mississippi after a shooting. According to Nate, Calloway was lucky to be alive. His manner seemed straightforward, his hand-shake firm, and his gaze direct. Veda liked him at once. An outsider with no preconceived opinions and biases seemed a good choice to take lead on Tony Redmond's murder case.

"I've heard a lot about you, Dr. Campion. Webber County is lucky to have you."

"Thank you, but as my uncle said, I'm only here temporarily until Dr. Bader returns."

"I'm trying to talk her into a more permanent arrangement," Marcus said. "But that's for another day. Nate, could I have a word?"

The two wandered off leaving Veda alone with Calloway. She got right down to business. "Anything I need to know before I exam the body, Detective?"

"Only that this looks to be a bad one, though maybe not too shocking for you. Coming from New Orleans, you probably saw this kind of thing on a regular basis. I know we got our share in Memphis."

"I saw a lot of things that I hope to never get used to," she said. "What do you mean by *a bad one*? Can you be more specific?"

He gave her a look she couldn't define in the dark. "It's been my experience since moving down here that the ho-micides in this county are almost always drug-related or else a domestic dispute that gets out of hand. Or both. This one appears to be a professional hit. Deliberately planned and carried out in cold blood."

She tried not to outwardly react but instead casually lifted a hand to tuck back strands of hair that had blown loose in the breeze. "I would agree that a gunshot wound to the back of the head hardly seems random or impulsive."

"Take a close look at his wrists. Do they look banged-up to you?"

"Ligature marks?"

He nodded. "Which means he was likely restrained before he was shot."

"Even if he was, that doesn't preclude a drug deal gone bad." Veda's gaze flitted to a shadowy corner of the cemetery where her uncle and brother watched from a distance. Why had Nate not told her about the marks when he called earlier?

"I'm not ruling anything out at this point," Calloway said. "What I do know is that Tony Redmond was a big guy. An ex-jock from what I'm told. A local football hero."

"That was a long time ago."

"Looks like he kept himself in shape. I remember seeing him in town a few days after his release and thinking his biceps looked to be the size of small hams. Apparently, he spent a good deal of his time in prison pumping iron. Given his strength and size, he wouldn't have been easy to take down or tie up unless he was first subdued. I'm betting he was either drugged or ambushed from behind. Look for signs of blunt force trauma."

"Given the poor lighting and the amount of blood I see on the ground, that determination might have to be made after we get him cleaned up."

The detective gave another brief nod. "The postmortem will be critical in this case. The sooner we get that report, the better."

"One step at a time," Veda said. "Right now, I need to examine the body, and my team needs room to photograph and video the process."

"In other words, you want my team to back off. I get it. You have your investigation, and we have ours."

"Cooperative but independent," she agreed. "It's the only way to ensure that nothing comes back on either office. No loopholes for a clever defense attorney to exploit regarding methods and techniques."

He said approvingly, "That's an admirable goal, considering the history your family has with the deceased."

She glanced at him in surprise. "You know about that?"

He shrugged. "I used to spend summers down here with my grandparents. People talked back then, and they talk now. From what I can tell, camps are still divided. Some think he did it, a few still swear by his innocence. We may never know the truth now." He glanced back at the body. "One thing I do know. If I were in your shoes, I might find objectivity a little hard to come by."

She echoed her uncle's sentiment. "You don't need to worry about that. This case will be treated as any other."

"Then, the scene is yours, Dr. Campion."

At some point while she'd stood conversing with Detective Calloway, her brother and uncle had gone their separate ways. She thought at first Nate had taken her advice and left the scene altogether. No such luck. He'd only retreated deeper into the shadows. She could see him just beyond the reach of the portable light. She couldn't make out his expression, but she sensed the intensity of his stare. Her scalp prickled a warning. Earlier, she'd been worried about Owen's alibi, but now she was starting to wonder about Nate's.

She shifted her gaze away from her brother and reminded herself to focus. *Just do what has to be done.*

Gripping the handle of her case, she approached the deceased as Detective Calloway observed from the perimeter.

Blood had pooled on the ground beneath the body, and the sight gave her pause even though she was no stranger to crime scenes. This was different. The victim's identity challenged her concentration. Her mind kept wandering back to Lily. How could it not? She was only human, after all.

Her uncle was right. Given the circumstances, this would be a big case for Webber County. Lots of speculation, lots of media attention. The role she and her family played in the investigation would likely come under intense scrutiny. It was imperative that she remain in control of her emotions and perform her duties to the best of her abilities. No mistakes. No lapse in judgment. Not a single shred of evidence could be overlooked because of carelessness or lack of focus.

She set her case on the ground and snapped on a pair of latex gloves as she nodded to the two waiting morgue attendants. "Ready?"

First, she stated her name and credentials for the video, followed by the date, time and location. She took a few moments to draw a verbal sketch of the immediate scene and the condition of the body. Her voice shook a bit in the beginning. She didn't think anyone else would notice, but she cleared her throat and started over.

Don't think about the victim's name. Don't think about what he did. Forget, momentarily, the last images you have of Lily. This is a crime scene like any other. You know what to do. Take readings. Collect samples. Protect the hands. Fill out the paperwork and you're finished.

She continued the commentary for the video as she felt for a pulse, a routine precaution regardless of the mortal wound at the back of his head. Then she checked for rigor mortis, lividity and insect infestation, all of which would help establish time of death and determine whether or not the body had been moved. She took measurements and the body temperature, collected blood and gun residue samples and examined the bruises and abrasions around the victim's wrists. Then she covered his hands with paper bags to preserve evidence that might be trapped on the skin or beneath the nails.

Before she closed her kit and turned the scene over to Detective Calloway, she filled out the forms and tags that would be secured inside the body bag during transport to the morgue. *No mistakes. Everything by the book.*

She nodded to Detective Calloway, who moved in eager to discuss her findings. She waited for her uncle to join them so that she didn't have to repeat her conclusions.

"He hasn't been out here long," she said. "The body is still flaccid. Cooling but not cold, and the blowflies haven't yet found him. I'd say two to three hours at the most."

"That would put time of death around midnight," Calloway said. "The kids who discovered the body called 9-1-1 just after. They were partying on the other side of the cemetery for a couple of hours before they decided to drive around to the front. They must have been here at the same time as the killer."

"They didn't hear a gunshot?" Veda asked.

"I've talked to them. They claim they had the music turned up too loud."

"It's also possible the shooter used a silencer," Marcus offered.

"Unlikely," Calloway said. "The location is remote. Why go to the trouble of obtaining a noise suppressor?"

"That's interesting," Veda mused. "They didn't hear the

killer, but if the music was turned up that loud, he must have heard them."

Calloway looked interested. "Meaning?"

"Why would he take the time to remove the restraints around the victim's wrists?"

"That's a damn good question, Dr. Campion."

"No one noticed a vehicle parked in the area or leaving the cemetery?" she asked.

"They came in through the rear gate. The suspect would have been long gone by the time they circled around to the front gate. That's when they spotted the victim. They got out of the car to see if he was still alive."

"Can you isolate their footprints from any other fresh prints?" Veda asked.

Her uncle answered the question. "Even if we could, it wouldn't help much. People are in and out of this cemetery all the time. There was a memorial service here just this afternoon." He nodded in the direction of a fresh grave. "Lots of people, lots of footprints. A procession of cars in and out of both gates."

"Do you think the killer was aware of the recent foot traffic?" Veda asked. "Maybe that's why he picked this spot."

"I have a couple of theories about the location," Calloway said, but he didn't elaborate as he turned back to the deceased. "I'll let you know when you can remove the body."

She nodded and stepped away from the immediate area to give the detective and his team room to work. Nate sauntered over as she and her uncle watched silently from the sidelines. He looked tense and pale in the harsh glow from the portable lights. "What did you find?"

"Time of death was likely around midnight," her uncle interjected.

"That's not what I mean." His gaze was still on Veda. "You kept focusing on his hands. What were you looking for?"

"I was trying to get a better look at the marks around his wrists," she explained.

He looked surprised. "What marks?"

"You didn't see them earlier?"

"Would I be asking for clarification if I had?"

She hesitated. "Weren't you the one who told me to do what needed to be done and then back off? Shouldn't you take your own advice?"

"Just answer the question, Veda."

"No, she's right," Marcus said. "You need to get the hell out of here and let Garrett do his job."

"How am I stopping him?" Nate demanded as he turned his back to the scene. "What marks, Veda?"

She glanced at her uncle who gave an exasperated sigh before he nodded. "He has what looks to be ligature marks around his wrists."

"Ligature marks?" Nate sounded incredulous. "As in, someone tied him up?"

"Detective Calloway thinks Tony was somehow incapacitated—possibly drugged or from a blow to the head—before he was brought out here."

"Did you see any other marks or wounds on the body that would corroborate his theory?" Nate asked.

"Not yet. We'll have a better idea of what happened once we get him cleaned up and on the slab."

"Let's go with Garrett's theory for a moment," Marcus said. "Someone knocked Redmond out, tied him up and brought him all the way out here to kill him. Before leaving the cemetery and with a bunch of kids partying within earshot, he then took the time to remove whatever had been used to restrain the victim's hands. Why?"

"Maybe he was worried about leaving something trace-able behind," Nate suggested.

"That was my thought, too," Veda agreed. "We may be able to determine the nature of the bindings once we get those bruises under a magnifier."

"Will you let me know what you find out?" Nate asked.

Marcus cut in impatiently. "Plenty of time to worry about that later. Right now, someone needs to go and see your mother. We won't be able to keep this under wraps for long, and I'd hate like hell for her to hear about the shoot-ing on the news."

"What about Tony Redmond's next of kin?" Veda asked.

"I'll handle the official notifications. You stay with the body, and Nate, you go talk to your mother."

Before Nate could protest, a car door slammed out on the street, and they turned in unison toward the sound.

"Let's hope someone hasn't already blabbed to the press," Marcus muttered.

But it wasn't a reporter who walked through the ceme-tery gates. Veda caught her breath as the newcomer strode down the designated path, pausing as he caught sight of the body illuminated by the floodlight.

Jon Redmond. The man who had worked tirelessly for nearly two decades to free her sister's killer.

Chapter Three

Veda tried to remember the last time her path had crossed with Jon Redmond other than from a distance. If memory served, their final confrontation had been outside the courtroom at his brother's trial. He'd only been twenty at the time, barely four years older than she, but the hard set of his stare and the harshness of his words had sent a chill straight through her heart.

She felt a similar sensation now as she stared at him in the dark with thunder rumbling in the distance and his murdered brother's body mere feet away. The years melted until she was back in that courthouse. She could still hear the raw anguish in his voice when he'd confronted her in the hallway, demanding to know why she'd lied on the witness stand. The accusation had shocked her, and she'd found herself responding with equal fire.

"I didn't lie! Everything I said in there was the truth."

"But not the whole truth. You said Lily confided in you that she was seeing someone behind my brother's back. But she never mentioned a name? She never even hinted at his identity? Come on, Veda. You must have some idea who he is."

"I don't. She wouldn't tell me. She said..."

"*Don't stop now. What did she say?*"

"*The timing had to be right because a lot of people could be hurt by the truth. Especially Tony. She was worried about how he would react when he found out.*"

That's not what you said under oath. You said she was afraid of how he would react. Words matter, Veda. There's a difference between fear and worry. What else did you get wrong?

"*Now you're just trying to confuse me.*"

"*No. I'm just trying to get at the truth. It never occurred to you that Lily's secret lover could have killed her?*"

"*Then, why was the murder weapon found in Tony's truck?*"

"*Someone could easily have planted it. All I know for certain is that he would never have hurt Lily in a million years. He's been in love with her since ninth grade. My brother isn't a killer, and if it takes the rest of my life, I'll find a way to prove it.*"

Owen had been standing nearby that day, and he'd leaped to Veda's defense as the conversation had grown more heated. He'd shoved Jon aside and threatened to punch him in the face if he ever so much as looked at his sister the wrong way. Even at fourteen, her kid brother had been a firebrand. Loyal to a fault, quick to temper and never one to shy away from a fight. That was Owen. Luckily, Nate was used to cleaning up their younger brother's messes. He'd dragged Owen from the courthouse to cool him off, but not before a handful of onlookers had gotten an earful.

The episode in the hallway was only one of many clashes that summer. The whole town became divided over the outcome of the trial. Everyone had an opinion and a theory. Despite the damning evidence presented at trial, Tony Redmond retained his share of ardent defenders, those vocal few who refused to see him as anything other than the local golden boy destined for greatness. A once-in-a-generation football hero with enough talent and star power to put Milton, Mississippi, on the map.

After Veda's testimony, rumors began to surface about her sister. Whispers of drug use and promiscuity. Veda blamed herself for the attack on Lily's character. Her testimony about a secret relationship had stoked a firestorm of speculation that threatened to taint the memories she had of her beautiful, brilliant, complicated sister. Lily had been no angel. She'd had her flaws and foibles just like everyone else. To the outside world, she was a beauty queen and an honor student, as dazzling in her own way as Tony Redmond. But to those closest to her, she could be emotionally distant and prone to dark moods that sometimes lasted for days. And her fear of thunderstorms bordered on the neurotic. In other words, her sister had been human.

Veda took a long breath as she let those memories and her cursory knowledge of Jon Redmond wash over her. After his brother's conviction, he'd returned to Ole Miss to finish his undergraduate studies and later his law degree. Veda could remember seeing him in town only a handful of times after Tony's incarceration. On those rare occasions, they never spoke or so much as acknowledged the other's presence. That wasn't unusual considering their history. They hadn't been friends even before the murder. He'd graduated the year before she entered high school. Like most people in Milton, Veda had known him as Tony Redmond's older brother.

Now a few other things came back to her about Jon Redmond. He'd been smart, reserved and a talented athlete in his own right, but his sport had been baseball in a state where football reigned supreme. He'd never been flashy or popular like Tony. However, from what Veda could tell in the dark, he'd aged into his classical good looks. She felt an odd prickle at the base of her spine. She and Jon Redmond had never been anything more than acquaintances, and yet their lives had been irrevocably entwined since Lily's murder.

He walked over to the deceased and crouched. The cops that had been milling about gave him space. It seemed to Veda that the night had grown preternaturally silent. Where were the crickets and the nightbirds? Even the CSI team worked with quiet efficiency in the background.

Head bowed, he remained motionless for the longest time beside his brother's body. Veda might have thought he was deep in prayer, but there was something about the rigid way he held himself that seemed at odds with a spiritual invocation. She couldn't help wondering what he was thinking. What he was feeling. If, as Nate had suggested earlier, he regretted his part in getting his brother released from prison. Veda was no stranger to guilt. She knew only too well the destructive nature of self-blame and second-guessing.

As if sensing her scrutiny, he glanced up. She could have sworn their gazes locked before he rose and nodded to Detective Calloway.

Marcus muttered something under his breath.

Veda frowned. "What did you say?"

"I didn't expect him to get out here so quickly. I'd hoped the body would be moved before he arrived."

"You called him?" Nate asked incredulously.

"No way around it. I had to."

"You could have gone to see Theresa Redmond instead," Nate said. "At the very least, you could have discouraged a visit to the crime scene. It's distracting having him here."

Distracting was an understatement, Veda thought.

"Look, son." Marcus put a hand on Nate's shoulder. "I know how you feel about Jon Redmond. I don't like what he did any more than you do, but he's not just the victim's brother, he's also the DA. He has a right to be here. Which is why I'm going to go over there and talk to him. It's my duty, and it's also the decent thing to do. You two stay here and keep quiet. Let me handle Jon Redmond."

"What do you think?" Nate asked as Marcus stepped away.

She turned to study his profile. He was staring after their uncle, his expression inscrutable. "About Marcus calling Jon Redmond?"

"About all of this," he said with a shrug. "Like it or not, it takes you back to that summer."

"I know. Lily's been on my mind ever since you called." She wrapped her arms around her middle and shivered at the distant growl of thunder. "Remember how frightened she was of storms? Earlier in the evening, there wasn't a cloud in the sky, and now this. It's like she's trying to tell us something."

He gave her a troubled look. "You don't really believe that, do you?"

She sighed. "Not really. As much as I'd like to think our loved ones can send messages from beyond, I'm too pragmatic. When you're dead, you're dead. But that doesn't stop me from missing her."

"I miss her, too." He let down his guard for a moment and a note of melancholy slipped in. "Not a day goes by that

I don't think about her. I still have spells where the murder keeps me up at night. I'll lie in bed and wonder what her last moments must have been like. How scared she must have been. I was her big brother. I should have protected her."

"We all wish we could have protected her." Veda put her hand on his arm but only for a moment. Neither of them was comfortable with demonstrative gestures. "I'm the one with a reason to feel guilty. All those terrible things that were said about her were because of me. I broke her confidence. I betrayed her trust."

"You told the truth under oath. No one can fault you for that. Besides, who cares what people said? Most of them didn't even know her. As for blame, the only person truly responsible for what happened to our sister was Tony Redmond. We both need to remember that. And tonight, he got what was coming to him."

Veda couldn't help but flinch at his brutal summation. "Do you ever wonder…?" Her gaze flicked away.

"Wonder what?" Nate demanded.

She regretted almost instantly her train of thought. Tony Redmond killed her sister. No one else. The evidence against him may have been circumstantial, but it was overwhelming. He slit her throat with a utility knife he used for work, and afterward he threw the bloody weapon in the back of his truck, either unconcerned about being caught or still out of his mind with rage. Then he drove to the nearest railroad crossing, parked across the tracks and waited. A passerby saw his truck on the tracks and found him slumped over the steering wheel. Unable to rouse him to unlock the door, the man managed to push the vehicle to safety in the nick of time. The police concluded it was a murder–suicide gone wrong. Two wasted lives, and all because Lily had told Tony Redmond she didn't love him anymore.

"Do you ever wonder what her life would have been like if it hadn't been cut short?" Veda improvised. "I like to think she would have found happiness, but those dark periods took a toll. And those nightmares she had. They started after we lost Dad, and she never outgrew them. I loved her dearly, but sometimes I wonder if I ever really knew her."

"People are complicated. She was always Dad's favorite," he said without rancor. "His accident was bound to have had a profound effect. As for the moods…sometimes there's no rhyme or reason. Maybe it was just the way she was wired."

"I guess." Veda's gaze strayed back to Jon Redmond. He was still conversing with their uncle, but his attention seemed to be elsewhere. He wasn't looking at Marcus or his brother's body. Instead, his head slowly turned as his gaze raked the cemetery, probing corners and shadows as if he sensed something amiss or an unwanted presence. For some reason the notion made Veda uneasy. "I wonder what they're talking about."

"His brother was shot dead tonight. What do you think they're talking about?" Nate paused. "Don't look now, but you're being summoned."

Her uncle motioned her over as he called out her name. "Veda? A word?"

She closed her eyes briefly before squaring her shoulders. Speaking with the bereaved was the hardest part of her job. Speaking to Jon Redmond would be even more difficult.

"Just be cool," Nate said. "And for God's sake, don't say anything about the fight, even if Redmond brings it up."

"Why would I? Owen is home in bed asleep. No reason to believe otherwise."

Nate gave her a long stare as she repeated his earlier assertion. "That's right. Now, you better go. Marcus looks like he could use backup."

She joined her uncle and Jon Redmond reluctantly.

"Jon, you remember my niece, Veda Campion. Tonight, she's Dr. Campion."

Jon met her gaze straight on. "Of course I remember you."

His voice had deepened since they'd last met, and there was a note of something that might have been disdain around the edges. Possibly her imagination. Their history would naturally influence her perception. One thing she knew for sure: the stare was the same. The intensity caught her off guard, and for a moment she found herself back on the witness stand.

During her testimony, she'd wanted to look her sister's killer straight in the eyes, make him flinch or glance away in guilt. Instead, her attention had strayed to the first row of spectators directly behind the defense table. Jon Redmond had leaned across the railing to whisper something in his brother's ear, but his gaze never left her. She'd been struck by the electric blue of his eyes and for a moment had floundered helplessly until the prosecutor came to her rescue and repeated the question. Later, he told her that she'd done fine on the stand, particularly for someone her age, but until the guilty verdict came back, she'd been certain that her lapse had cost her credibility with the jury.

She wasn't that same nervous sixteen-year-old now. Jon Redmond's blue eyes had no power over her. She'd been called to testify on numerous occasions during her time with the Orleans Parish Coroner's Office, and she'd quickly learned to control her nerves and hone her poise. A penetrating glare couldn't faze her.

Still, she was relieved when he didn't offer his hand. She stood with her arms at her sides as she nodded a greeting. "I know how difficult this must be for you. I'm sorry for your family's loss."

A retort leaped to the tip of his tongue—she was almost certain of it. His mouth thinned, and his jaw hardened a split second before he glanced toward his brother's body and then closed his eyes on a shudder.

In that fleeting moment, the world seemed to stop for Veda. The voices in the background faded, the harsh floodlight dimmed, and a rush of emotion took her by surprise. She was suddenly keenly aware of Jon Redmond's grief, punctuated by the scent of the cemetery roses that grew along the fence. She had the strangest urge to touch his hand, to weave her fingers through his in an illogical gesture of solidarity, but the impulse passed quickly. When his gaze returned to Veda, still with that glare, she wondered if she'd imagined his vulnerability.

"I understand you've already examined the body and come to a conclusion regarding time of death."

"Midnight," Marcus stated conclusively.

Veda was a little less absolute. "Going by how little the body has cooled—as well as other factors—I'd put time *since* death no more than two hours. Three at the most."

"What are those others factors?"

She shot a glance at her uncle, but he remained passive, arms folded, rocking back slightly on his heels. She turned back to Jon. "Pale but flaccid skin, clouded corneas, rigor mortis in the small muscles of the face that hasn't yet progressed to the limbs. We'll know more after the autopsy. Stomach content can be especially helpful—" She stopped herself from getting too graphic. They were talking about his brother, after all. "I'm sure as DA you're aware of the various tests and procedures that will be performed during the postmortem."

"Yes, I get the picture." He was silent for a moment. "My brother was shot in the back of the head. Here." He lifted a finger to his crown.

"Approximately," she agreed.

"Point-blank range, would you say?" His voice was carefully controlled, though she thought she detected a slight tremor now and then.

"I noticed what might be singeing and muzzle burn around the entrance wound, but it's difficult to say for certain until the body is examined under better conditions. If I'm right, that would certainly indicate contact or near-contact. You should also know that he has bruises and inflammation around both wrists."

He gave a brief nod. "Detective Calloway mentioned the marks. Was my brother on his knees?"

The question caught Veda by surprise, though she supposed it was a logical conclusion. "I'm sorry?"

"He was shot at close range with his hands likely bound behind his back. Was my brother forced to his knees before he was executed?"

Executed. The word hung between them for the longest moment until Veda broke the tension. "It's possible. We'll know more about trajectory, velocity, caliber and ballistics after the autopsy."

"When will that be?"

"Dr. Bader will be back sometime tomorrow...today.

I'm sure he'll make this case a priority. You could have a preliminary report by early afternoon. Toxicology will take longer, possibly a few days depending on the backup at the lab."

Again, he nodded absently, his thoughts apparently elsewhere. "The tox screen needs to be comprehensive, not just a routine check for blood-alcohol content. Look for traces of GHB, Rohypnol or ketamine, to name a few."

"Knockout drugs," Marcus said. "Any reason in particular you think someone dosed him?"

"My brother was a fit man. He was strong, and he knew how to fight. He couldn't have been taken down under normal circumstances."

"Detective Calloway reached the same conclusion," Veda said. "Although, he thinks Tony might have been ambushed from behind."

Marcus shot her a look as if warning her not to say too much. She was reminded again of the fight between her brother and Tony Redmond. Tony had been bigger, but Owen was quicker. He'd more than held his own.

"Did your brother have any enemies?" Marcus said. "I'm sure Detective Calloway has already been over this with you, but I'm asking again. Can you think of anyone who wanted Tony dead?"

"You mean other than a Campion?"

There it is, Veda thought. He was already making assumptions about her family.

Marcus said in a tense voice, "I wouldn't go throwing around accusations until we have all the facts."

"Everybody in town knows Owen attacked my brother without provocation." His gaze shifted to Veda as if he expected her to come to her brother's defense. She wanted to, but under the circumstances she thought it best to keep her mouth shut. "However, I'm not accusing anyone…yet. My brother was behind bars for a long time. You don't survive nearly two decades in a maximum-security prison without making both friends and enemies."

"You have someone specific in mind?" Marcus pressed.

"No." But a slight hesitation made Veda think he wasn't being altogether forthright.

Marcus shot her another glance before he continued. "Word has it someone was in town a few days ago asking questions about Tony. A guy by the name of Clay Stipes. I made some inquiries. He lives over in Kerrville. Turns out he served time with Tony up at the farm. You know anything about him?"

"I know the name," Jon said. "They were cellmates for a few months after my brother's incarceration."

"No idea why he came to town looking for Tony?"

"All I know about him is what my brother told me."

"Which is?"

"He's a convicted cop-killer," Jon said.

Marcus looked grim. "I heard that, too. I also heard he's hiring himself out as a PI, which is probably a front for any kind of service his client is willing to pay for."

"A private detective?" Jon sounded genuinely surprise. "How was he able to get a license?"

"Anyone willing to hire a cop-killer wouldn't care about a license. This guy…he's not someone you want hanging out around your family, particularly with your little sister home from college for the summer. She and your mother are out there all alone in that big house. I'd advise taking some precautions."

Jon's mouth tightened. "I'll watch out for them."

"You might want to watch out for yourself while you're at it. Stipes wasn't just looking for Tony. I hear he was asking around about you, too. You don't know anything about that, either, I suppose."

"I've never even met the man," Jon said.

"A guy like that can be unpredictable. Who knows what he's after? Like I said, you best take some precautions. You own a gun, by chance?"

"I don't need a gun to take care of myself," Jon said. "But thank you for your concern."

Was that a note of sarcasm? Veda wondered.

He gave her a curt nod before he turned and left the cemetery.

Veda watched him until he was out of sight. "That was uncomfortable."

"For him, too, I suspect."

"What was all that business about the ex-con? You think he had something to do with Tony's murder?"

Marcus shrugged. "Could be. The sheriff over in Kerrville says the guy's bad news. I doubt he came to town for a friendly reunion." He rubbed his chin as he stared down the path where Jon Redmond had disappeared. "I'd bet a month's pay he knows more than he's willing to say about Clay Stipes."

"I got that impression, too," she agreed.

Nate said behind her, "He's going to be trouble."

She hadn't heard him approach and whirled in surprise. "Who, Stipes?"

"Did you hear what I said?" He sounded tense.

Veda started to answer, then realized he was addressing

their uncle. The two men exchanged a look that, for whatever reason, made her blood run cold.

Marcus said in a resolved voice, "If there's trouble, I'll deal with it. Now, go home and keep your mouths shut until I say otherwise."

Chapter Four

Jon sat in his car unnoticed as the morgue attendants carried his brother's body through the gates on a stretcher. Veda Campion followed, but Nate and Marcus remained in the cemetery. Garrett Calloway hadn't come out yet, either. He'd identified himself as lead detective, but Marcus Campion had done most of the talking. Calloway might be the public face of the investigation, but Jon was under no delusions about who would be running things behind the scenes. For that reason, he needed to speak to Veda alone. He had no idea how she would react to his request, given the bad blood between the two families. If she was amenable, his proposal might provide a little healing, but he knew he was asking a lot.

He ran a hand over his eyes. Exhaustion and grief bore down heavily, and he wanted nothing so much as to retreat back to his apartment and sit alone in the dark with a good, stiff drink. But that would have to come later. Right now, he had to keep it together for a little while longer. His mother and sister didn't yet know about Tony, and that would be the toughest visit of his life.

He scrubbed his face and tried to think back to happier times before the incarceration. Sometimes those memories seemed more like dreams. His brother had been sent away for so long that he'd become a stranger to his own family, and in some ways his return had made all their lives more difficult. The adjustment hadn't been as smooth as any of them would have liked. Tony came out of prison a completely different person. He'd been a scared eighteen-year-old kid when he'd been sent up, and he'd walked out the gates a hard-scrubbed man who'd learned to survive in the oldest and cruelest penitentiary in Mississippi.

There had been times—more than a few—over the years when Jon had wanted to wash his hands of his brother's troubles. Just walk away and live his own life. But the one thing that had never changed was the certainty of his brother's innocence. He'd made a promise to Tony and to himself that if it was the last thing he ever did, he'd clear his brother's name.

He shook off the cloying cloud of despair and tried to focus. The morgue van was getting ready to leave. Veda handed a clipboard through the window before stepping aside to allow the driver to make a U-turn. Then she retreated to the back of an SUV, presumably to store her gear. The light came on when she opened the lift gate, and Jon took that as his cue.

He got out of his car and started down the road toward her vehicle. He didn't call out as he approached because he didn't want to attract unwanted attention. She was leaning into the cargo space and didn't seem to hear the crunch of his footsteps on gravel. Too late Jon realized that he'd caught her in a state of undress. She'd already discarded the paper jumpsuit along with her white T-shirt, and now she stood rummaging through a duffel bag in her jeans and bra.

She glanced around when he cleared his throat, then

froze in the glare of the interior light. Their gazes collided for a moment before she whirled back to the duffel bag and grabbed a shirt. With a muttered oath, she jerked it over her head and down over her bra.

"Sorry," he murmured as he tried to gauge her reaction. He'd only had a glimpse of her expression before she turned away, but he thought she looked more surprised than angry.

She cut him a look over her shoulder. "What do you think you're doing?"

No, he was wrong. He heard plenty of anger in her voice now and no small amount of contempt. He tried to fix the situation with another apology. "I'm sorry. I didn't mean to catch you off guard."

"Then, you shouldn't sneak up on me in the dark," she snapped, as she tugged the tail of her shirt down over her jeans and then reached up to adjust her ponytail. Only then did she turn to face him.

She was taller than Jon remembered. Or maybe her rigid posture only made her seem so. She was also more attractive than he remembered. Not the bombshell her sister had been even at eighteen, but he had no doubt Veda Campion turned more than a few heads. Under other circumstances and without their history, he might have had a greater appreciation for her good looks, but his brother had been murdered only a few hours ago. At the moment, he didn't give a damn about anyone or anything else. He tried to tell himself he was only searching for answers, but the simmering rage that boiled just below the surface spoke to a baser need that might have been revenge.

He took a deep breath and tried to calm his racing thoughts. He was here for a reason. Confronting Veda Campion with old wounds and unwarranted suspicions would only drive her away.

"I thought you left." She sounded calmer now, but she was still yanking at the hem of her T-shirt as if worried she might remain exposed.

He told her the truth. "I came out here to wait for you."

That got her attention. "Why?"

"I was hoping we could have a moment alone." He could see her clearly in the glow from the interior light. Her eyes widened in surprise, followed by a quick frown of disapproval.

"Shouldn't you be with your family?"

He felt a stab of guilt at her query. She knew how to cut to the quick. "I'm on my way there now." He paused to take a breath. "First, I need to talk to you about something. It's important."

She lowered the lift gate so the light wasn't shining in their faces. He wondered if she'd put them in the dark on purpose because he couldn't read her at all now.

"I already told you everything I know. Dr. Bader will meet with you after the autopsy. He'll be able to answer your questions more thoroughly."

"The autopsy is what I want to talk to you about."

"I don't understand." Then revelation seemed to dawn, and she said in a crisp voice, "Oh, I see. You're worried about my involvement. Well, you needn't be. As I mentioned earlier, Dr. Bader will handle the postmortem. This is my last night on the job. As soon as he clocks in, I'll be officially unemployed."

"You won't stay on to assist? Or at least to observe?"

"There's no reason for me to." She opened the lift gate again and began to fiddle with her bags and equipment, undoubtedly hoping to draw the conversation to a close now that she'd put his concern to rest.

He said carefully, "You misunderstand me. I'm asking you to be present."

"At the autopsy? Why?"

"I have my reasons."

"I'm sure you do." She kept her back to him as she finished her tasks. He couldn't see her expression, yet the disbelief and suspicion in her voice confirmed what he already knew: this wasn't going to be easy. "Why do I get the feeling you're working up to something that I'm not going to like? What's this really about?"

"Two pairs of trained eyes and hands are better than one," he said with a shrug.

She gave him a sidelong glance. "That's all there is to it?"

He hesitated. "Dr. Bader's ability to perform a conscientious exam worries me. He's not as sharp as he used to be. He misses things. Cuts corners. His carelessness has caused problems in a few of my cases. I don't want to take a chance that something gets overlooked or forgotten during my brother's autopsy."

She leaped to her colleague's defense as he figured she would. "I think you're selling the man short. I've known Dr. Bader for years, and early on in my career I considered him a mentor. He's always been a skilled pathologist."

"How long has it been since you observed his work firsthand?" Jon kept his tone even. He didn't want to push back too hard and drive her away before he'd laid all his cards on the table. "He should have retired years ago, yet he continues to overextend himself. Are you aware that several surrounding counties have contracts with the Webber

County Coroner's Office to perform a certain number of autopsies per month?"

"No, but I'm not surprised. We did the same in Orleans Parish. Coroners in smaller and poorer counties and parishes don't always have the necessary facilities or training to perform postmortems."

"Dr. Bader also conducts a fair number of private autopsies. Families pay him out of pocket when state law doesn't require a postmortem."

"Also not unusual. Even if death is from natural causes, loved ones need answers and a measure of closure," she said. "Performing private autopsies is neither illegal nor unethical. It's part of the job. Unless you're suggesting that Dr. Bader is somehow getting kickbacks. In which case, where's your proof?"

"I don't have any," he admitted. "All I know is what I see, and his work has gotten sloppy. I need someone in that autopsy room I can trust."

"And you trust me?" She sounded shocked.

He answered without hesitation. "I do. Despite past scandals in the Orleans Parish Coroner's Office, you left with your reputation intact."

"How would you know that?"

He had to feel his way through what could turn out to be a minefield. At that moment, he was all too aware of their history. All too cognizant of the fact that one wrong word could bring the conversation to an abrupt end and crush any chance he had of enlisting her help. "It might surprise you to learn that I've followed your career from time to time."

Wrong tact. She all but physically recoiled. *"Why?"*

"Not for nefarious purposes," he was quick to assure

her. "Although, I can see why you might jump to the wrong conclusion given our last meeting."

"You mean the one where you accused me of lying under oath?"

"I shouldn't have done that," he said. "I've long since regretted it."

She waved aside his concession. "I'm over it. Besides, let's not get distracted. Tell me why you, of all people, would be inclined to follow my career?"

"Long story short, the law firm I worked for in Atlanta before I came here had an office in New Orleans. I was sent down to do background research on a murder case. You were on the witness list. I was surprised when I read your name. I didn't think there could be two Veda Campions, so I did some digging."

"I'm sure you did."

He managed a smile. "You wouldn't have done the same?"

She merely shrugged.

"I found out you were a highly respected pathologist in Orleans Parish. And after I watched you take the stand in that case, I understood why. You were not only poised and knowledgeable but also relatable. You explained everything in terms the jury could understand without talking down to them. That's not easy. Everyone on my team was impressed."

"That's odd," she said. "Because I'm pretty sure I would have remembered seeing you."

"I was only there to observe, so I sat at the back. I didn't come up to you afterward because… You know how it is."

She lifted her chin. "Yes, I do know how it is. Which is why I find this whole conversation so puzzling. From accusations of lying to singing my praises. I can't help but wonder why."

"I told you. I want you to assist or at the very least observe my brother's autopsy."

"Still not buying it," she said bluntly. "There has to be more to it than that."

"I'm being straight with you. I intend to do everything in my power to find my brother's killer and bring him to justice, and I'm asking for your help."

"There's just one problem with that request." She folded her arms. "What makes you think I'd want to help you?"

"Because I believe the person who killed my brother also killed your sister."

JON REDMOND'S RIDICULOUS claim kept playing over and over in Veda's head as she left the cemetery and drove to the morgue. All these years after her sister's murder, he was still trying to proclaim Tony's innocence. She wanted to be compassionate enough to give him quarter on the night of his brother's murder, but this was nothing new. From the first, his insistence that Tony had been framed had been so convincing that even Veda had found herself playing the what-if game from time to time. She'd always been able to talk herself down by remembering certain facts. Tony Redmond had been found with the murder weapon in his truck and Lily's blood all over his hands. The right man had been sent to prison, and earlier tonight, justice had been cruelly served.

Dread welled inside Veda as she clutched the steering wheel. She took deep breaths and told herself to get control of her emotions. She was preoccupied and driving too fast. The streets were empty, but that was no excuse. Easing up on the gas, she glanced in the rearview mirror, almost expecting to find Jon Redmond in hot pursuit.

Had he really thought she would agree to help him? After the pain and grief his family had caused hers? She'd been so flabbergasted by his suggestion that she'd stood tongue-tied and flushed with indignation. Finally, she'd sputtered, "You can't be serious!"

To which he'd replied, "I'm dead serious. Your sister's killer is still out there somewhere. Tonight, he murdered my brother to cover his tracks. I won't rest until I bring this person to justice."

"What tracks? Lily was murdered a long time ago. If someone else was involved, the evidence would have come to light by now."

"You know that isn't true. Has her mystery man ever been identified?"

She'd gaped at him in outrage. "Are you still dwelling on that?"

He'd gone silent as if realizing he needed to back off and regroup. "I know this has come as a shock—"

"Not so much shock as utter disbelief. You're living in a fantasyland. You're grasping at straws, trying to make sense of what happened tonight, and I get that. But leave me out of it."

"I can't. You're the only one who can help uncover the truth. You knew Lily better than anyone."

"I'm not sure that's true," she murmured.

"Look." He ran a hand through his hair. "I realize this isn't time or place. You still have work to do, and I need to be with my family. But I'd like to talk to you again. Soon. Alone. Can we meet somewhere?"

"I don't think so. I'm sorry for your family's loss, and

I'm truly saddened for what you all are about to go through. But I can't help you. This crusade of yours... I don't want any part of it. You're right about one thing, though. I still have work to do, and it's already been a long night. So goodbye, Jon."

Not *Good night* but *Goodbye*. She wanted to believe the finality of her farewell would be the end of it, but she didn't think getting rid of Jon Redmond would be that simple. Obviously, he wasn't a man easily dissuaded. *You don't devote seventeen years of your life to a cause only to take no for an answer.*

No matter his resolve, he couldn't force her to help him. She wasn't worried about holding her own against him or anyone else, for that matter, but she was more than a little curious about his ulterior motive. He wasn't telling her everything about his intentions just as he hadn't come clean about Clay Stipes. There was more going on than met the eye, and now that her assignment at the coroner's office was coming to an end, she would have plenty of free time on her hands to do some digging.

Not that she'd ever throw in her lot with Jon Redmond. That would never work. The past would always color their individual perspectives, making consensus impossible. However, nothing prevented her from conducting her own investigation. She was good at piecing together puzzles. She did it every day at work.

As Jon had been so quick to remind her, the man Lily had been involved with that summer had never been identified. Veda had always wondered about him, about why he hadn't even showed up to the funeral or the graveside service to pay his respects. But maybe he had. Maybe Lily's secret lover was someone familiar, someone whose behavior and demeanor hadn't given him away even in the face of a tragic loss. Someone closer than Veda could ever have imagined with secrets of his own to protect. And with the kind of insight into Lily that no other living person on the planet could offer. He was still out there somewhere, still keeping his secret. Maybe it was high time he came out of the shadows.

A shiver trailed down Veda's spine, mostly from excitement but with a measure of trepidation. Digging up the past might come with a cost. The possibility of physical danger seemed remote and didn't particularly worry her. The real fear came from the things she might uncover about her sister that would change her perception forever.

She pulled into her temporary parking spot at the morgue and got out. Using her key card to enter the bleak facility, she signed in at the desk and then checked to make sure the decedent had been properly processed. She compared the name and number on the cold cabinet with the corresponding paperwork she'd filled out at the scene. Satisfied that everything was in order, she signed back out and left.

Outside the facility, she stood for a moment searching the sky. The storm seemed to have fizzled into nothing more than distant and sporadic flickers of lightning.

Hey, Lily. If you were trying to tell me something earlier, I missed the clue.

She folded her arms around her middle and shivered. The clouds were starting to thin, but the breeze that blew through the live oaks still felt charged. Maybe the storm hadn't passed after all. Maybe it had stalled in the distance, building strength.

Climbing into her vehicle, she stared absently into the darkness before she shook off her mood and started the engine. She didn't go straight home but instead turned in the opposite direction from her bungalow.

The square of blocks east of downtown—recently redubbed the Warehouse District—had once been a bustling industrial area. Most of the factories and warehouses had been shuttered for decades, but a few had been converted into lofts and apartments, a real estate venture that had once seemed like a pie-in-the-sky scheme. With the influx of newcomers to the area, the district had become more urbanized and desirable, though with a seedy edge that put Veda on guard as she drove through the narrow streets still lined with deserted buildings.

She pulled to the curb across from a brick-and-sheet-metal monstrosity that had once been a shirt factory. Owen lived on the third floor in the corner unit. The windows in his place were dark, but that wasn't unusual at this hour. She would have been more concerned if all the lights had been blazing.

Fishing her phone from her bag, she punched in his number and waited. She expected to see a light go on the moment her call went through, but her brother's windows remained dark, and he didn't answer until the fourth ring.

"Veda? What's wrong? What's happened? Is it Mom?"

He'd jumped to the same conclusion she had earlier, and she was quick to put his mind at ease. "She's fine. So is Nate. This isn't about the family."

"Thank God." She heard him let out a heavy sigh of relief. "What's up?"

"Something's happened. Let me say again the family is fine. But we need to talk. It's important."

He sounded puzzled and mildly annoyed. "Okay, but do you have any idea what time it is?"

"A little after four in the morning."

"And you couldn't wait until a more decent hour?"

"This won't take long. I'm parked across the street from your building. Can I come up?" He hesitated for so long, she wondered if the call had dropped. "Owen? Are you there?"

"I'm here, but I'm not there." His tone had altered slightly, though Veda acknowledged the shift might be her imagination. She hadn't noticed that cautious note when he first answered.

Even so, her fingers curled around the phone in consternation. "Where are you?"

"I'm at Ashley's."

Ashley Duquesne had been his on-again, off-again girlfriend since high school. Veda had once chastised him for stringing her along for so many years, unwilling to make a long-term commitment. *Not that it's any of your business, but what makes you think I'm the one dragging my feet?* She'd made a point to stay out of his personal life after that.

"Have you been with her all night?"

Another hesitation. "She's working the graveyard shift at the hospital. I'm here alone at her place."

Veda wondered why he hadn't gone home to his apartment. "What time did she go in?"

"Her car is in the shop, so I dropped her off around nine. Her shift didn't start until ten, but she wanted to go in early and get a jump start on paperwork. What's this about anyway— Wait a minute. You said this wasn't about family. Ash—"

"This isn't about her, either. She's fine as far as I know." Veda heard a door open and close. "Are you alone?"

"I just told you. Ashley's at work."

"That didn't answer my question."

"I stepped out on the balcony for a minute. What the hell is going on, Veda? You wake me up at four in the morning to find out if I'm alone?"

She drummed her fingers on the steering wheel as she stared out the windshield at a car parked up street. For whatever reason, she took note that it was a dark colored sedan. "I know it doesn't make sense yet, but there's a reason for all these questions. I need to see you in person, Owen. Does Ashley still live in the apartment complex off Holcomb? I can be there in five minutes. Meet me outside."

"Veda—"

"Meet me outside, Owen."

She severed the call before he could protest. Throwing the phone onto the passenger seat, she started the engine, but her hand froze on the gearshift. She initially assumed the car down the street belonged to someone in the building. No one had come in or out while she sat there, yet now she could have sworn she detected a silhouette through the tinted glass.

Probably my imagination. It was still dark and she was more than a little on edge. It wasn't every day she was called to a crime scene to examine the body of her sister's killer. Not to mention the conversation she'd had with the killer's brother. She was tempted to drive slowly past the vehicle and peer through the driver's window, but instead she turned around in the street and headed the other way.

She kept track of the car in her rearview mirror. The sedan pulled away from the curb and fell in behind her, but the lights never came on. That definitely wasn't her imagination. She was being followed, and another unnerving thought occurred to her. Had the person behind her been watching her brother's apartment? Was she leading him straight to Owen?

At the next intersection, she turned right at the last minute. The vehicle behind her kept going straight, still without lights. She wanted to believe it was only a coincidence that the sedan had left at the same time as she. Maybe the driver had forgotten to turn on the lights. It happened. But she wasn't taking any chances. She took a circuitous route to meet Owen, keeping her eye on the rearview and peering down side streets.

Satisfied that she'd lost the tail—if she had indeed been followed—she pulled into the apartment complex and parked at the back of the lot. When Owen came out of the building a few minutes later, she flashed her lights. He answered with a wave, then wove his way through the parked cars to climb inside her vehicle. He was fully dressed but his hair was unkempt, and his shirt looked like he'd slept in it. That wasn't so unusual for Owen. For a handsome guy, he didn't put a lot of emphasis on appearance.

Unlike Jon Redmond. His image popped into her head for no good reason. Despite the late hour and the circumstances, he'd been well-dressed and groomed at the cemetery except for a thick stubble. He'd looked exhausted but pulled-together.

She forced her attention back to Owen. Apart from the gauze he'd wrapped around his banged-up knuckles, he appeared to be fine. She was relieved to note that he didn't seem particularly stressed or wired but instead looked puzzled and more than a little aggravated.

He slammed the door and turned. "What the hell, Veda?"

She killed her engine and shut off the lights. "I'll explain everything. Just give me a minute." She adjusted the rearview mirror so that she could see the entrance to the parking lot. No one came in or out. She scanned the rows of parked cars. Nothing amiss there, either. Her brother might not be nervous, but she certainly was.

Leaning back against the seat, she tried to relax. It would be dawn soon. She wondered about Jon Redmond and whether or not he'd broken the news to his family yet.

"What are you looking for?" Owen demanded.

"Just checking to make sure I wasn't followed."

He looked at her as if she'd taken leave of her senses. "Are you okay?"

"It's been a strange night."

"Apparently so. Okay, I'm game. What makes you think you're being followed?"

She glanced out her side window. "I may be overreacting, but when I was at your place just now, I noticed a car parked at the curb across from your building. A black or possibly dark blue sedan. The driver pulled out behind me when I left, but he didn't turn on his headlights."

"Probably someone looking to score drugs," he said without much concern. "That area isn't nearly as safe as the developers and real estate agents would have you believe."

"And something tells me you're okay with that."

He gave her a little smirk. "I've never minded a few rough edges. Gives me an excuse to keep up with my target practice."

She sincerely hoped he was joking. "Can I ask you a question?"

"Why stop now?"

"Did you come straight back here after you dropped Ashley at the hospital? You said around nine, right? That's early for you."

"That used to be early for me, but fine. I'll answer your question when you tell me what the hell is going on."

"I'm getting to that. Just humor me, okay?"

He dropped his head to the back of the seat with a heavy sigh. "Let's see. I stopped and got gas at a corner store. Bought some breath mints while I was there. You know, the kind that comes in the little pink tins they keep near the register. Then I dropped by a sports bar and had a beer—domestic—while I caught the last few innings of the game. The Braves won, in case that was going to be your next question. I left around ten thirty and came back here."

She ignored his sarcasm. "Did you run into any acquaintances at the bar? Anyone who might have noticed what time you left?"

"It was Sunday night so the place was pretty empty." He checked his side window as if her nerves had rubbed off on him.

"Did anyone see you when you came back here? Someone in the parking lot, maybe."

"I have no idea." He turned to stare at her expectantly. "Your turn now."

She nodded and got right to the point. "Tony Redmond was murdered earlier tonight. His body was found in Cedarville Cemetery a few hours ago."

He sat in silence for a moment. "You know this for a fact?"

"I was called to the crime scene. I just signed his body into the morgue. Yes, I know this for a fact."

Another moment of dead silence. Then he said, "Do the cops have any idea who shot him?"

A cold chill went through Veda. She returned her brother's stare for the longest moment before she said in a hushed voice, "I never said he was shot."

"I think you did."

"No, I didn't."

Owen shrugged. "Well, that's what I heard. Besides, it's the logical end to a guy like Tony Redmond."

He'd done his best to gloss over the slip, but Veda wasn't buying it. Her heart started to thud as a dark thought poked and prodded. "Tell me the truth, Owen. How did you know he'd been shot?"

He gave her an enigmatic look. "How do you think I knew?"

Her fingers curled around the edge of the seat. "You didn't just take a wild guess. You seemed too sure."

"So, that's why you're here." He studied his bandaged knuckles. "That explains the third degree. You think I did it, don't you?"

"I don't know what to think. Just tell me how you knew about the shooting."

He turned to meet her gaze, a sly smile curling the corners of his mouth. "Nate called while you were on the way over here. He told me about Redmond."

She reached over and punched his arm. "You jerk. Why didn't you say so?"

"Ouch! I wanted to know what you were building up to with all those questions. Admit it. I had you going. You already had me tried and convicted there for a minute."

"That was cruel, Owen."

"If it's any consolation, you scared the hell out of me when you called. You're good at this interrogation business. A little too good."

"I'm just asking the same questions the police will likely ask if and when they come knocking on your door."

His good humor vanished. "Why would the cops want

to question me? I've been here all night. I didn't have anything to do with Tony Redmond's murder."

"Don't be naive," she scolded. "You had a very public and very vicious altercation with Tony just a few days ago. You're still wearing a bandage on your knuckles from that fight. There were witnesses besides me who heard you threaten to kill him."

"That was in the heat of the moment," he protested. "It didn't mean anything."

"The police may not see it that way. Given our history with Redmond, they could take that threat very seriously. It doesn't help that no one can vouch for your whereabouts at the time of the murder."

"You're forgetting something pretty important," he countered. "Our brother is a detective, and our uncle is the chief of police."

"The case has been assigned to another detective. Nate's been shut out. As for Marcus, he can't do anything that so much as hints at meddling or a cover-up without risking his reputation and maybe even his job."

"They'll have my back." He sounded so sure of himself, she wanted to punch him again. He trailed his finger through a fine layer of dust on the dashboard. "Don't you ever clean this thing?"

"Don't change the subject." She grabbed his hand and examined the bandage. Fresh blood oozed through the gauze. "Owen, you're bleeding."

He pulled free and rested his hands on his thighs. "I keep knocking the scabs off at work. The damn things won't heal."

"You should wear gloves. Or hire some help." Her brother was in the landscape business. He and his partner still did most of the manual labor themselves. "Soil contains a lot of bacteria. Tetanus, salmonella and E. coli, to name a few. You don't want to risk an infection."

"Ash gave me an ointment and a week's worth of antibiotics. I'll be fine."

"Prescribed antibiotics?"

She could almost hear his eyes rolling. "Jeez, Veda. Now you're the pill police?"

"I'm just trying to help."

"I appreciate it but ease up a little. You're starting to sound like Nate. He lives to pick at every little thing I do."

"Why? What did he say when he called?"

"Pretty much what you did. He told me about Tony, and then he said I should lie low for a few days. But I can't do that. I have a job."

"Hopefully, an arrest will be made soon, and you won't have to worry," Veda said. "Until then, Nate's right. You need to keep your head down. And maybe think about talking to an attorney. You don't want to get caught by surprise and blurt out something that could be used against you."

He gaped at her.

"Okay, maybe an attorney is overkill at this point," she conceded. "But you know what they say. *Hope for the best and prepare for the worst.*"

"Wouldn't hiring an attorney just make me look guilty?"

"The police will try to make you think it does, but you shouldn't let that influence your decision. A good attorney can guide you through an interrogation and keep you from saying anything incriminating."

He stared at her in disbelief. "You're serious about this."

She shrugged. "Take it with a grain of salt. According to Nate, I have a tendency to make mountains out of molehills. I sincerely hope that's what I'm doing, but I have a bad feeling about this." She thought about her conversation with Jon Redmond and wondered about his true motivation for trying to enlist her help. If he could get her to let down her guard, maybe he thought she would say or do something that could be used against her family.

"It's your decision," she told Owen. "And Nate could be right. Maybe all you need to do is lie low until this all blows over."

"Ash's brother-in-law is a lawyer. I guess I could run it by him. Get his take."

"That sounds like a good idea."

"Thanks, Veda."

She said in surprise, "For what?"

"For the advice. For coming over here. For having my back."

"Did you think I wouldn't?"

He seemed to consider his answer. "You've been gone for a long time, and you haven't been all that great at keeping in touch. I guess I wondered if you were still one of us."

"Phones work both ways," she said. "So does the interstate. How many times did you visit me in New Orleans?"

His sly look returned. "There was that one time during Mardi Gras."

"You mean the time you and your friends trashed my apartment while I was at work, and I saw you all of five minutes the whole weekend?"

"Yep, that time." He got out of the vehicle, then turned to say through the open door, "It's good to have you home. I hope you decide to stick around for a while. Maybe you can help Nate keep me in line."

"That's a big job. I don't know that I'm up to the challenge," she teased. "Get some rest. We'll talk later."

She drove away from the apartment complex wishing she felt better about their conversation. They'd ended on a light note, but something unpleasant still simmered beneath the good-natured banter. Owen had been able to set her mind at ease about his prior knowledge of the shooting and the fresh blood on his bandage, but there was no glossing over the fact that he didn't have an alibi for the time in question.

Veda didn't want to think the worst of her brother, but no matter how many times she reassured herself that he wasn't a killer, the fight with Tony Redmond kept rearing its ugly head. She'd never witnessed anything like it. The savagery in her brother's eyes had shocked her. In the space of a heartbeat, he'd morphed into a stranger, one who seemed only too capable of taking a human life.

Chapter Five

Dr. Bader agreed to meet with Jon late that afternoon to present his preliminary findings from the postmortem. All the way to the morgue, Jon wondered if he would run into Veda. If by some miracle she'd changed her mind about helping him. But he didn't see her SUV in the lot when he pulled up, nor did she show up for the meeting. Not that he had expected her presence. The Webber County Coroner's Office was very much Dr. Bader's domain.

However, even a brief appearance in the hallway would have signaled that she was at least willing to hear him out. Unfortunately for him, her absence also sent a message. He liked to think it was just a matter of timing. She'd been adamant that her assignment ended with Dr. Bader's return. Maybe she hadn't wanted to step on the elder pathologist's toes.

Or maybe he was grasping at straws again. He'd done that a lot over the years when all hope seemed lost. Sometimes clinging to a lifeline, no matter how fragile, was the only thing left to do.

As much as he'd wanted a second set of eyes in the autopsy room, he had to admit Dr. Bader's summation was clear and concise. He'd answered all of Jon's questions and had seemed in no hurry to usher him out. Despite the coroner's thoroughness, however, little surfaced in the preliminary report that Jon didn't already know or at least suspect.

The downward trajectory of the bullet from the entrance wound corroborated his theory that Tony had been forced to his knees before he'd been shot at close range with a 9 mm weapon. The marks around his wrists had been made by a plastic strap, possibly a heavy-duty zip tie. Law enforcement often used self-locking zip or flex ties instead of standard handcuffs when making mass arrests because they were easy to carry and disposable. But there were dozens of everyday uses, everything from bundling wires and cables to staking tomato plants, and they could be bought over the internet or in any hardware or big-box store.

Dr. Bader's preliminary report was just that—an abbreviated rundown of the findings from the autopsy. Additional information such as ballistics and toxicology could take days.

Jon left the building with a nagging headache and an unpleasant hollowness in his chest. He'd been up since seven the previous morning—thirty-three hours straight—with little more than coffee and a piece of dry toast to keep him going. He felt strung out from exhaustion. A shower and shave might have boosted his morale, but he didn't have time to swing by his apartment. Not yet. There was still too much to do. People to call. Arrangements to be made. If he could close his eyes for even a minute, he might feel like a new man when he awakened, but he couldn't allow himself even that small luxury.

At four in the afternoon, the sun still beat down relentlessly on the asphalt parking lot. As he strode toward his car, he wondered if he should take the time to at least stop somewhere for a quick bite. He couldn't keep going for much longer on caffeine and resolve, but the thought of food left him queasy. He needed to get back to his mother and sister anyway. The news of Tony's death had been devastating, as he'd known it would be. His mother had tried to put on a brave face for Gabby's benefit, but Jon was worried about her. How much grief and heartache could one person suffer before something had to break?

Earlier when he'd left the house for his appointment with Dr. Bader, she'd walked him out to the porch and placed a hand on his arm. "Do you have any idea who did this?"

"No, but I'm going to find out."

Her fingers had tightened around his arm, and her voice quivered with emotion. "Jonny, please be careful."

She hadn't used his nickname since he was a kid. He'd hugged her tight for a very long time, trying to offer comfort and reassurance while secretly relieved that he had somewhere to go, a purpose that allowed him to escape the heavy oppression of grief in the house for even a few hours.

The headache throbbed as he approached his vehicle. He'd managed to snag a space in the shade, which would make climbing inside the hot car only a little less hellish. As he unlocked the door, he automatically scanned his surroundings. Tony wasn't the only one who had enemies. DAs couldn't be too careful these days.

He felt a warning prickle at the back of his neck a split second before he saw someone standing beneath the heavy limbs of the same live oak that shaded his car. The man appeared to be watching him, but his faded jeans and gray T-shirt camouflaged him so well that for a moment, Jon thought the afterimages in his eyes from the glaring sun might be playing tricks on him. Then the man called out his name.

"Jon Redmond?"

He relocked his car and checked his periphery as he walked toward the stranger. "Can I help you?"

The man made no move toward him but instead allowed Jon to come to him. "Do you know who I am?" he drawled.

Jon paused in the deep shade as his gaze raked over the stranger. "I have a pretty good idea."

Clay Stipes grinned, using his tongue to shift a toothpick to the other side of his mouth. He looked to be somewhere in his midforties, at least six feet tall and solidly built with wide shoulders and bulging biceps. *Stout* was the word that came to mind. *Formidable* was another. His hair was dark, his complexion leathery, and his voice had the kind of raspy quality that came from years of smoking. When he turned to observe a passing car, Jon saw the jagged whiteness of an old scar running along his jawline from ear to chin.

He slipped a hand in the pocket of his trousers, letting his fingers close around his phone just in case. "What are you doing here?"

Stipes leaned against the tree trunk and folded his arms as if he didn't have a care in the world. "I heard about Tony. Thought I'd stop by and pay my respects."

"At the morgue?"

"I happened to be in the area."

Sure he had. He'd undoubtedly followed Jon here, which meant Stipes must have been staking out his mother's house. "How did you find out about my brother?"

He bent his left knee and flattened his foot against the tree trunk. "We were supposed to meet up last night. A little honky-tonk Tony knew about out on the highway. Far enough from town so as not to attract unwanted attention but close enough to the action to make things fun. Lolita's." He drew out the middle syllable, giving the name a lascivious pronunciation. "I waited awhile, had a few drinks. When he didn't show, I figured something had happened. I started poking around and found out about the shooting. Tough break." He pushed himself off the tree trunk and took a few steps toward Jon. "All those years he spent behind bars only to get shot dead when he came back home. That must rile you up. I'd be out for blood if he was my brother. How's your mother holding up?" he added without missing a beat.

Jon said with undisguised contempt, "My mother doesn't concern you."

He shrugged. "Just being polite."

"What were you and my brother meeting about?"

"We had unfinished business to discuss." Stipes removed the toothpick from his mouth and pointed it at Jon before flicking it away. "Now you and I have unfinished business."

"I don't think so. Whatever agreement you had with my brother is now null and void."

"That's not the way I see it." Stipes squinted as a thin shaft of sunlight broke through the oak leaves and caught him in the eye. He stepped back into the shade. "Where I come from, honoring your brother's debts is the gentlemanly thing to do."

"I'm no gentleman," Jon said. "And more to the point, I don't have any money."

"Just barely making ends meet on a lowly public servant's salary, is that it? Yep, been there." He removed another toothpick from his shirt pocket and clamped it between his teeth. "I happen to know you can get the cash. I've done some checking. Your family owns property all over the county. What you didn't sell off to pay Tony's legal bills is worth a lot of money these days, what with all the snowbirds moving down here. You've got more than enough to pay your brother's debt and have a nice little nest egg leftover."

"Most of that property belongs to my mother, not me."

"That's what Tony said, but like I told him, I'd rather not involve her in any of our dealings if we can help it. Keep it between us and let the poor woman grieve in peace."

Jon glanced back at the street, automatically checking his surroundings before elevating the confrontation with Stipes. Then he said slowly, "Maybe it hasn't had time to sink in yet or maybe you're just that dense, but whatever leverage you had over my brother is gone. He can't be sent back to prison, so there's nothing you can do to hurt us that hasn't already been done."

Stipes cocked his head. "You sure about that?"

"I'm sure about this. The police know who you are. They've already linked you to my brother. If you're smart, you'll slink back to where you came from before they come looking for you."

The man's grin thickened. "Thanks for the heads-up, but I kind of like it here. Nice town if you don't mind all the murders. I plan on sticking around for a while."

"Suit yourself." Jon turned to walk away. "That'll just make you easier to find."

Stipes said behind him, "Did Tony ever tell you how we met? It's a good story. I think you'll find it interesting."

Jon started to keep walking, but something in Stipes's

voice compelled him to turn. "You shared a cell. That's hardly riveting."

"Before that. We crossed paths when he first got off the bus. He was just a green kid back then. Scared spitless like all the other fresh fish. He wouldn't have lasted a month at the farm without someone watching his back."

"And I suppose you were that someone?" Jon asked with no small amount of sarcasm.

"I knew my way around. A cop has to learn pretty fast on the inside who he can trust."

"Don't you mean *former cop*?" Jon eyed him with open derision. "I'm pretty sure they confiscated your badge and gun when you killed your partner."

Stipes didn't seem offended. He said with a shrug, "Son of a bitch had it coming. He agreed to cut me in on the little side business he had going, then he set me up. It was him or me that night. Lucky for me, I had enough information that allowed my attorney to cut a deal. I turned state's evidence against his—let's call them *associates*—and in return, I got a reduced sentence. Twenty years, out in ten for good behavior."

"I don't need your whole life story," Jon said. "Why did my brother come looking for you?"

"He heard I had connections on the outside, heard I had a knack for digging up things. People. Information. He wanted help finding out who killed his girlfriend. You know the drill. Claimed he was innocent. Swore he was framed. Oldest story in the book among convicts. They're all innocent to hear them tell it. But your brother was different."

Jon's attitude subtly shifted. "You believed him."

"Say what you will about how things turned out, but I was once a damn good cop. I knew how to read people.

The kid was earnest. But he had a lot of pent-up anger that was going to get him in trouble and maybe me, too, if we didn't find a way to channel his rage. I agreed to help him for a fee to be paid when we both got out."

"I'm sure you found a way to make it worth your while in the meantime."

"Let's just say the partnership was mutually beneficial. I wasn't running a charity, after all. Your brother," he said and pointed with the toothpick again, "he toughened up real quick inside. After a while, nobody dared mess with us. He had my back, and I had his."

"Meaning you used him for muscle."

"He was young, strong. All that anger had to go some-where. And he wasn't afraid to get his hands dirty. I'll say that for him."

Jon had a sudden image of his brother behind bars, fighting for his life, always looking over his shoulder. He'd downplayed the violence over the years for their mother's sake and maybe for Jon's, too. But his scars told a different story. "And these outside connections of yours?"

Stipes nodded. "They were mainly law enforcement. Buddies I'd worked with in the past. A couple of cousins still on the force. I put out some feelers, and a few days later the information started to trickle in."

"What did you find out?" Jon hated that he'd been so readily hooked. He was starting to see how his brother had gotten mixed up with a guy like Stipes. Despite all the rough edges, he could be persuasive.

"His girlfriend wasn't the angel everyone thought her to be," Stipes said.

Jon frowned. "Lily?"

"Turned out another of my cousins knew her—or at least,

knew of her. She used to drive over to Kerrville where she wouldn't be recognized to buy drugs and party. Sometimes, she brought her boyfriend with her. Not Tony. This guy was older, maybe thirty, thirty-five at the time. They both went to great pains to conceal their identities, but a girl like Lily Campion attracts attention. I've seen pictures." He gave a low whistle. "People got curious and started asking questions. Someone who knew someone had a friend who knew someone…that type of thing. Turned out, the guy was married, and his old lady came from money. He had a lot to lose if word got out about his teenaged girlfriend."

"Who is he?" Jon asked. "Does he still live around here?"

The grin flashed again. "So I finally have your attention."

"Did Tony know the man's name?"

"Tony knew everything I knew and then some. He wasn't just my muscle. The kid was smart. Once he had time to think things through, he started putting two and two together."

"If that's true, why wouldn't he have told me? Or his attorneys?"

"Think about it," Stipes said. "Why would he? What could you do about it without hard evidence? Besides, if you started nosing around in the guy's business, you would've tipped him off. That was the last thing Tony wanted. He planned to confront the guy himself."

"How was that going to work with him in prison?"

"He said you'd get him out. The kid was sure of it."

Jon felt a well of emotion at the revelation. He wasn't sure he'd been worthy of his brother's blind faith. How many times had he wanted to give up and walk away?

He swallowed past the lump in his throat and hardened

his tone. "Let's talk about the here and now and the opportune way you turned back up in my brother's life. I'm guessing you heard he was out, and you came looking for money. When he had a change of heart, you threatened to go to the police with a made-up story about a murder-for-hire scheme."

"Who says it was made-up? Your brother and me, we had a deal." Something ugly gleamed in Stipes's eyes.

"Even if that's true, it just means you took advantage of a desperate young man who'd been wrongfully sent to prison. When he got out and couldn't or wouldn't come up with the money, you shot him."

"Why would I kill him?" Stipes spat out the toothpick. "He's not worth anything to me dead."

"Except here you are trying to shake me down." At that moment, Jon was only too aware of the kind of person who stood mere feet away from him. An ex-con and a cop-killer who had thought nothing of trying to blackmail his brother.

Stipes feigned surprise. "You think this is a shakedown? This is just business. I'm a private detective, in case you hadn't heard. I get paid to dig up information for my clients."

Yes, but what else do they pay you for? "Whatever you're calling it these days, I'm not interested," Jon said flatly.

"Maybe not yet. Maybe you haven't hit enough brick walls."

"Maybe I just don't like dealing with the person who threatened my brother."

Stipes appeared unthwarted. "Ask yourself this. Why is it you haven't been able to uncover in seventeen years what I was able to dig up in a matter of days from a prison cell?"

"I'm sure you're just dying to enlighten me," Jon said.

"It's simple. Someone like you doesn't have what it takes to do what it takes."

"And how would you know that?" Jon countered. "You don't know anything about me."

Stipes looked him up and down. "I know all I need to know just by looking at you. The way you dress. The way you carry yourself. You think you can find the information on your own? Get back to me when you've been elbow-deep in a ripe dumpster or up to your knees in the sewer. Even then—" he gave Jon another once-over "—the people you need to talk to wouldn't give someone like you the time of day. Like it or not, you need me. I can help you take this creep down. That's what you want, right? Think it over for a day or two and get back to me. You can find my number in Tony's phone."

"The police have his phone."

"The other phone." He gave Jon an enigmatic look. "You've got a lot to learn about your brother. This should be fun."

VEDA SPENT HER first afternoon of unemployment with her mother. They took care of several projects around the house and then worked out in the garden until the heat drove them to the shady back porch. Her mother poured home-made lemonade from a frosty pitcher and served gingersnap cookies on a blue willow plate. The simple treats took Veda back to her childhood when she used to spend so much time with her grandmother. She held the chilled glass to her overheated cheek as she tipped her head to the breeze from the ceiling fan. I could get used to this, she thought. I might even be happy here.

They rocked in companionable silence for the longest

time until her mother finally broached the subject of Veda's future plans, and then her pleasant mood vanished.

"I haven't made any decisions yet." She dusted cookie crumbs from her fingers onto a paper napkin. "I've had offers. I'm taking some time to mull over my options."

"It just seems a bit impulsive, and that's not like you." Her mother gave her a worried glance. "You said you took a leave of absence to be with family, then you up and quit your job for good. But instead of staying here with me, you rent a place in town as if you plan to be here for a while. Not that I don't love having you close, but I can't help wondering what brought on this sudden change of heart."

"Nothing," Veda said with a shrug. "I really did come back home to be with family. I knew with Tony Redmond getting out of prison and living here in Milton, you'd be under a lot of stress. I wanted to make things easier for you. I rented my own place because you and I are both too set in our ways. We would have driven each other crazy living under the same roof. You know it's true," she insisted when her mother started to protest. "As far as quitting my job, it wasn't all that sudden. I've been thinking about a change for a while now. Between school and work, I've lived in New Orleans for well over a decade, and as much as I love the city, I'd like to stretch my wings. See what else is out there for me."

Her mother let her say her piece, then asked quietly, "Does this need for a change have anything to do with the doctor you were dating last Christmas?"

"Adam? Of course not."

"I was sorry to hear things didn't work out. You seemed so well-suited."

"Turns out we weren't," Veda said. "We both worked

long hours and rarely saw one another. It was easier to go our separate ways."

"Easier for you or for him?"

"It was a mutual decision, Mom."

Her mother frowned as she stared out over the garden. It was an idyllic setting with butterflies dancing through the lantana and honeybees busy in the coneflowers. If Veda let her mind drift, she could almost see Lily out there picking roses.

"I've often wondered why none of you kids has ever married," her mother mused.

Veda turned in surprise. "Really? What's to wonder about? It seems perfectly normal to me. We're all busy building careers and living our lives."

Her mother wouldn't let it go. "You're all in your thirties now. You should be settling down, buying homes. Raising babies of your own."

"That's your dream, not mine." Veda gave her an accusing look. "Are you suddenly pining to be a grandmother? Is that what this is about?"

"I don't know how sudden it is." Her mother tucked back a stray lock of hair. "I won't deny a desire to have children running around this place again, especially now that I'm retired and have time to enjoy them. But this isn't about me. I'd hate for you to miss out on what your dad and I had. We married young, some might say too young, but I never regretted a minute of it. I never felt like I missed out on anything. He was the love of my life."

"I know, Mom. But I'm not you."

Her mother didn't seem to hear her or chose not to. "After the accident, I didn't know how I would find the strength or the will to go on without him. The guilt and grief were almost unbearable."

"Guilt?" Veda found herself enthralled in spite of herself by her parents' tragic love story. "What did you have to feel guilty about? You were devoted to Dad."

"I walked away from the same accident that claimed his life. You don't think I still ask myself why him and not me?" She sounded more pensive than anguished.

"It was an accident. No rhyme or reason."

"It was an accident, yes, but I'm the one who wanted to drive home in the middle of a rainstorm. You were so young when it happened. I don't know how much you remember, but we'd gotten a call from your grandmother a few days earlier. That was before she moved down here. She'd fallen ill and needed my help. Your dad dropped everything and drove me to Tennessee so that I could take care of her. I'd never spent the night away from you kids and it pained me to leave you for a day, much less a whole week. As soon as your grandmother was on the mend, he came back for me. Instead of waiting until the following morning as we planned, we set out that night. Maybe it was a premonition or maybe I was just being an overprotective mother, but I felt a very strong need to be home."

Veda had heard the story before, but she didn't try to stop her mother's memories. Sometimes a person just needed to get these things out. After the passage of so many years, the accident that claimed her father's life still weighed on her mom.

"I'll never forget that rain," she murmured. "It came down so hard we had to pull over a couple of times, and we saw lightning strike a tree. We were almost home when a truck veered into our lane. Your dad swerved, but the car skidded on the slick pavement. It all happened so fast, and in the silence after the crash, I remember thinking what a close call we'd had. And then I looked over and saw your dad…" She sighed. "The image is still vivid after all these years."

"I'm sorry, Mom."

She was still in her own little world. "I wallowed in that guilt and grief for weeks, barely able to get out of bed, but then I realized how much my misery would have pained him. He would have wanted me to pick up the pieces and get on with my life. Find a way to be happy again. Besides, I had four kids to raise. I had to be strong."

"I don't know how you did it," Veda said. "We were a handful."

"Your grandmother moved down a few months later. She was a godsend, but you kids were what saved me. You gave me a reason to get up in the morning. I thought I'd lived through the worst pain a person could ever go through, and then we lost Lily." She closed her eyes on a shudder. "No mother should ever have to endure that agony."

"I know," Veda said. "But maybe it's not good to dwell on all that sadness."

Her mother nodded. "You're probably right. I didn't mean to get maudlin. But I do have a point to all this. I sometimes wonder if the reason you and your brothers can't commit to a serious relationship is because you've been through so much pain and you're afraid of losing someone else you love."

There might have been some truth in her mother's theory, but Veda wasn't ready to concede. "Did you ever stop to think that maybe the right person hasn't come along yet? Maybe we don't want to settle. Besides, we've still got time. Except for Nate. He's practically an old man now."

Her mother cut her glance. "No. He just acts like one."

The tension lifted as they both chuckled.

Her mother sighed. "Don't mind me. I've been in a mood lately."

"Tony Redmond's release from prison put us all in a mood." Veda flashed back to Owen's fight with Tony. The ferocity of the attack. The verbal threat. And then the loaded glance between Nate and Marcus at the crime scene. She didn't think either of her brothers capable of murder— certainly not the cold-blooded, premeditated act that had claimed Tony Redmond's life—but something had been gnawing at her since Nate's phone call.

"Veda?" Her mother peered at her curiously. "Honey, are you okay? You seemed a million miles away just now."

She snapped back to the conversation. "Sorry. I was just thinking about something. What were you saying?"

"We were talking about Tony. I said it wasn't easy having him come back here. I avoided going places where I thought I might run into him."

"I did the same."

"I'll confess, though," her mother said as she traced a drop of condensation down the side of her glass, "now that he's dead, I'm ashamed of some of the thoughts that went through my head when I heard he was getting out."

"We've all had those thoughts." Veda set her glass aside and curled a leg beneath her. "But under the circumstances, we should allow ourselves a little grace."

"Maybe you're right. I can't help thinking about poor Theresa and what she must be going through."

"She's been on my mind, too."

"Despite everything, my heart goes out to her. I never

blamed her for what Tony did, but afterward, I couldn't bring myself to continue our friendship."

"No one can fault you for that." Veda really didn't want to talk about any of the Redmond family, but apparently her mother still had things she needed to get off her chest. Veda vowed to spend more time with her. She obviously had a tendency to brood when left alone with too much time on her hands.

"We had so much in common back in those days," she said with a sigh. "We were both widows raising large families on our own. I remember how pleased we were when Tony and Lily started going out. We prided ourselves on the fact that we didn't have to worry because we'd each brought up such good kids. And they were so beautiful together. Do you remember? Everyone thought of them as the perfect couple."

"Until they weren't," Veda said bluntly.

"Until they weren't," her mother repeated softly. "Sometimes I wake up in the middle of the night, and I still can't believe it happened. The Tony I knew could be full of himself, but he had a good heart. At least, I thought so. I look back now and think how could I have missed the signs? How could I not have known what that young man was capable of?"

"None of us knew. Something just snapped in him that night. But this is a very depressing conversation," Veda said. "Maybe we should talk about something else. Or better yet, why don't you go inside and cool off in the air-conditioning? I'll pick up the garden tools and put them away."

"I am tired," her mother admitted. "I haven't been sleeping well lately."

"Then, go lie down and take a nap. I'll finish out here."

"Will you be here when I get up?"

"Yes, go on." Veda waved her inside. "I'll just putter around the house until it's time to fix dinner."

She cleaned the shovels and clippers and stored them in the garden shed. Backtracking to the porch, she carried the glasses inside and rinsed them at the kitchen sink. She wiped down the counters and took out the trash, and then she went upstairs and stood in the open doorway of Lily's old room.

Hovering on the threshold, she let her gaze roam over the familiar space. Nothing much had changed in the years since her sister's death. Her mother swore she hadn't kept the room as a shrine or a memorial or anything like that. Raising four kids on her own had simply made her cautious about finances. Why spend good money on new furnishings when the old was still perfectly fine?

The furniture, bedding and linen curtains were all the same, but the band posters had been removed, and the walls had been painted a soft lavender. The subtle color deepened in the afternoon sunlight, giving the room an almost ethereal air that was at once dreamy and a little unsettling. If she closed her eyes, she could see her sister peering in the vanity mirror or sitting on her bed with schoolbooks spread all around her and a phone to her ear. She could hear Lily's favorite song in the background and those heart-tugging whimpers in the middle of the night.

Who were you, Lily? Why do I feel as if I never knew the real you?

Veda wandered around the room, touching trinkets on the dresser, lifting a forgotten candle to her nose. Finally, she went over to the closet and opened the door.

Lily's clothes were all gone. Her mother had tucked away

the items she wanted to keep in tissue-lined boxes and do-
nated the rest to a women's shelter. Photo albums and other
mementos had been neatly stored in airtight containers on
the top shelf. Other than those few plastic bins, the space
was empty. Even the hangers had been removed.

Veda was thinking of sorting through a few of the old
photographs, but instead she turned off the light and moved
to the deepest corner of the closet. Lowering herself to the
floor in the dark, she leaned her back against the wall as
she drew up her knees.

Memories floated like ghosts through the cramped space.
She tried to resist the tug of the past, but exhaustion made
her sluggish and vulnerable. With a sigh, she rested her
head on her knees and gave in to the lure. She drifted back
in time, years before the murder, to the night when she'd
first discovered Lily's hiding space. It was storming outside. Veda had been too young to understand the depth
of her sister's fear but old enough to want to comfort her.
She'd gone looking for Lily after an especially loud clap
of thunder. She found her huddled on the floor at the back
of the closet with her hands pressed against her ears. Veda
had scooted in beside her, offering as much sympathy and
comfort as a child knew how to muster.

*"Don't worry. It's just a storm," she soothed. "It'll blow
over soon. Mom says thunder is always a lot farther away
than it sounds."*

*"But that's not true," Lily whispered back. "She only
says that to make me feel better. She doesn't know what
the thunder really means."*

"What does it mean?"

*Her sister raised tear-stained eyes and shuddered. "It
means the bad man is coming."*

Veda had no idea who or what the bad man was, but she knew enough to be frightened. She put a trembling hand on her sister's arm. When Lily recoiled, Veda jumped. "What bad man?"

"He doesn't have a name. All I know is that the thunder summons him. He climbs through my window and sits on the edge of my bed to watch me sleep."

Veda found enough courage to scrabble to the doorway and glance out into the bedroom. "No one's there."

"He'll come. I know he will."

Veda crawled back to her sister's side. "Maybe you just had a bad dream. I have them sometimes, too."

Lily said in a strange voice, "You should go back to your room. If you see him, pretend you don't know."

"Know what?" Veda had a bright idea. "Come back to my room with me. I'll lock the door. I won't let him come inside."

"You're just a little kid. You can't stop him."

"Yes, I can!"

Lily shook her head with a forlorn sigh. "Daddy is the only one who can keep me safe."

"But Daddy's gone. Don't you remember? He had an accident."

Lily hugged her knees tighter. "Of course I remember. I'm the reason he's dead."

The memory drifted away, leaving Veda gloomy and unnerved. She felt a strange combination of emotions. She hugged her legs and rested her chin on her knees. The walls of the closet seemed to close in on her, making it difficult to breathe. She attributed the panicky sensation to claustrophobia, but confined spaces had never really bothered her. The only place she'd ever felt real fear was the attic. One of her brothers had once locked her inside for an entire afternoon, though to this day, neither had ever confessed. They blamed her entrapment on a faulty door latch.

She told herself she'd done enough wallowing in the past. Poking and prodding at all those old memories just made her feel helpless and more than a little unnerved. She needed to get out of that oppressive space and leave the past where it belonged. After all these years, did she really think a memory or a photograph would help her to understand her troubled sister?

But even as she decided to go back downstairs and out into the garden, another memory crept on icy feet from the shadows of her subconscious. She tried to shove the unwelcome creature back into the darkness, back into her mind's lockbox, instinctively realizing that some memories were too painful—and maybe too dangerous—to be unleashed. But already she could hear Lily's whimpers.

It was the night of her sister's eighteenth birthday. The family had had dinner together with Lily's favorite red velvet cake for dessert. Afterward, she and Tony had gone to the movies. They'd graduated from high school a few weeks earlier, and on that fragrant summer night, the two of them seemed to have the whole world at their feet.

Veda had been sound asleep until a clap of thunder awakened her, and she lay for a moment, listening to the storm. She'd left a window open earlier and she could hear tree branches scraping against the side of the house. The sound grated, so she got out of bed and padded over to the window to glance out. She wasn't normally afraid of storms, but every once in a while, her sister's fear rubbed off on her. Tonight was one of those nights. She glanced over her shoulder almost expecting to find the bad man sitting on the edge of her bed.

No one was there, of course. She tried to shrug off her unease. It was just the storm. Nothing to be afraid of.

Lowering the window, she turned and left the room to tiptoe down the hallway to the bathroom she shared with her sister. The door to Lily's room was open, and Veda peeked inside. Her sister's bed was empty. It didn't look as though it had been slept in. Veda's first thought was that her sister hadn't come home yet, and she was going to be in a lot of trouble when their mother found out. Then she heard a strange keening sound coming from the back of the closet.

For the longest moment, Veda hovered on the threshold. She'd been fearless as a little kid, wanting nothing so much as to comfort and protect her big sister. Now she felt the need to protect herself, though she had no idea why.

Swallowing past an inexplicable terror, she'd slipped across the room to the closet door.

"Lily? You in here?"

"Don't turn on the light!"

A spidery sensation crawled up Veda's spine. Something in her sister's voice...

"Are you okay? The storm sounds worse than it is. It'll be over soon."

Nothing but silence came back to her.

She got down on her hands and knees and wove her way through a maze of shoeboxes to the back of the closet. Her sister sat rocking back and forth as she had years ago when they were children.

Veda said in a hushed voice, "What's wrong? Is it the storm?"

Lily drew a tremulous breath. "I saw him again."

"Who?"

"He came through my window and sat on the edge of

my bed. I pretended to be asleep. I've always been good at pretending. But I could see him in the flashes of lightning. He wore dark clothes, and he had red eyes."

Veda's heart was thudding by this time. "He isn't real, Lily."

"Then, why could I smell him?"

"You...smelled him?" Somehow the notion of an odor seemed the most horrific of all her sister's revelations.

"It wasn't bad like you would expect. It reminded me of Grandma's old cedar chest." She sounded puzzled. "That can't be right, though, can it? Shouldn't the devil smell like sulfur?"

Veda swallowed back her fear. She didn't know what to say, what to do. She had the strongest urge to scramble out of the closet and run back to her room, pull the covers over her head and pretend she didn't know about her sister's dream. Had never heard the awful keening that had sounded like a frightened kitten in distress.

Awkwardly, she rubbed her sister's arm as she'd done when they were little and whispered a litany of inane platitudes. "You just had a bad dream, that's all it was. The storm brought it on. You've always been afraid of storms. When you were little, you used to have the most awful nightmares. But you don't have to be afraid now. You're all grown up. Nothing can hurt you."

Lily shook her head sadly. "You don't understand. The nightmares went away a long time ago. I thought he'd gone, too, but now he's come back to punish me."

"Punish you for what?"

She sounded numb, distant. "I'm not the person you think I am, Veda. You shouldn't look up to me. If you knew the bad things I've done, you'd hate me."

The hair at the back of Veda's neck prickled. "What things?"

Her head lifted. "Can you keep a secret?"

Veda nodded.

"I shouldn't tell you. I promised I wouldn't say anything. But I can't keep it all inside anymore. Sometimes I feel like I'm going to explode if I don't tell someone."

"What is it, Lily? What did you do?"

She drew a shaky breath. "I've fallen in love with someone else. We're going away together."

Veda drew back in shock. "Who is he?"

"I can't tell you his name. It has to stay a secret for now. Tony doesn't know yet. Neither does Mom or the boys. You're the only one I've told. Promise me you won't say anything."

Her sister's confession rattled Veda. She tried to make sense of it. "You're going away? When?"

"I don't know. Soon, I hope. We haven't worked out the details yet."

"But I thought you loved Tony. You've been together forever."

"I'll always love Tony, but..." She made a sad little sigh. "Someday you'll understand. Or maybe you won't. I'm not so sure I understand it myself."

"You have to tell him. He'll be so crushed if he finds out from someone else."

"I will, but the timing has to be right. I don't know how he'll react. A lot of people could get hurt."

Veda wanted to nod in understanding, but at the moment, all she felt was keen disappointment. "Oh, Lily, how could you? He loves you so much."

"I know he does. Maybe too much."

Chapter Six

Veda couldn't take the gloom a moment longer. She scrambled out of the closet into the bedroom. Despite the cool air blowing from the vents, she went over and raised a window, drinking in the fresh air before shutting out the heat. Her mother found her a little while later sitting cross-legged on the floor of Lily's bedroom, surrounded by photo albums and yearbooks.

"I hope you don't mind." She waved her hand over the mementos. "I've been meaning to ask if I could take some of the photos back to my place and scan them."

"That's a good idea. I'd love to have digital copies for safekeeping." Her mother sat down on the bed and plucked at the trim on the coverlet as she glanced around the room. "I've been thinking again that it might be time to change things up in here. Maybe turn it into a sewing room. Isn't that what people do with spare bedrooms? Or a crafting space. Your grandmother's old sewing machine cabinet is still in the attic. Maybe I should have the boys carry it down for me."

"But you don't sew or craft," Veda pointed out. "You said you never had the patience for it."

"True."

She wondered if her mother had known about Lily's nightmares. Not that she was going to bring it up. They'd already spent too much of their visit on depressing topics, and Veda felt worn-out and worn down. "It's getting late," she said. "Should we go down and fix a bite to eat? I need to be getting home soon."

They ate chicken salad on crisp lettuce leaves with fresh strawberries and cantaloupe on the side. Veda stayed to help with the cleanup, then she headed out.

The sun had already dipped beneath the horizon by the time she turned down her street. The light softened as dusk crept closer, and something started to fret around the edges of her mind. She told herself she was just tired. Wandering around in all the old memories had taken a toll. Still, her guard was up. She didn't claim to be clairvoyant, but if there was one thing she'd learned from her time in New Orleans, it was to listen to her instincts.

A car was parked at the curb in front of her house. She thought at first it was the sedan she'd seen across the street from Owen's apartment, but the make and model were different. Nate drove a SUV similar to hers, and Owen owned a truck, so neither of her brothers had come for a visit.

She pulled onto the driveway and parked. Only then did she notice the man seated on her front steps. Jon Redmond waited until she climbed out of the vehicle before he rose to greet her.

Her pulse accelerated as she mentally braced herself and moved onto the brick walkway. She gave him a quick once-over, taking in the dark circles under his eyes and the lines of exhaustion that had deepened around his mouth. She would have sworn he had on the same clothes he'd worn to the crime scene at two o'clock in the morning, only now they were far from crisp, and he didn't seem at all pulled-together. The opposite, in fact. The day had obviously taken a toll.

She said, not unkindly, "You look like death warmed-over, and I would know."

He glanced down at his wrinkled shirt. "Sorry. I was on my way home to shower and change, but I thought I'd stop by here first. Maybe I should have done it the other way around."

"Or maybe you should have called first. How did you get my address, anyway?"

"I asked around. Milton hasn't grown that much." A hint of a smile flashed. "Everyone still knows everyone else's business."

She made no move to join him at the steps but instead kept her distance, slinging her bag over her shoulder and trying to act unmoved despite the tug of sympathy his haggard appearance evoked. "And?"

"And…" he spread his hands in supplication "… I apologize for showing up on your doorstep like this. I didn't think you'd take my call, and you no longer work at the coroner's office, so this seemed the best way to reach you."

"Why go to the trouble? As I understand it, the autopsy was performed earlier today. You've probably already seen a preliminary report."

"I have. But I'm not here about the autopsy. It was never just about the autopsy."

"Right." She gave a curt nod. "You think I know something about my sister's secret boyfriend. And that I withheld information about him on the witness stand. For what purpose, you haven't yet explained. But just to clear things up once and for all—had I known who he was, I would have shouted his name from the top of the courthouse steps."

He ran a hand through his hair, looking indescribably weary. "I don't think you deliberately withheld his name. I think you told the truth as you knew it. But you were just a kid when you were called to testify."

"I was sixteen. Hardly a child."

"That's young to go through the trauma of a murdered sibling." He paused, and she saw him draw a deep breath. "The trial was only a few months later. You must have still been devastated and grieving. We all were. But a lot of time has gone by since then. Sometimes things come back to us when we're no longer stressed. Or when we least expect it."

"Nothing has come back to me." Although, that wasn't exactly true. A lot of memories had surfaced during her time in Lily's closet. She'd always known about her sister's fear of storms, but she'd somehow managed to forget about the bad man in her nightmares. Maybe because even an imaginary demon crawling through windows and sitting on beds terrified her.

"The man she was seeing that summer may have been older, probably in his thirties," Jon said. "He may have been married. Supposedly, his wife's family had money. That could explain the need for secrecy. He had a lot to lose if the affair became public."

Veda looked at him askance. "He may have been this, he may have been that. And just where did these details come from all of a sudden?"

"I have a source who claims to know the man's identity."

"Oh, you have a source." Veda folded her arms. "Why do you need me, then?"

"He's not what I'd call reliable. To tell you the truth, I'm not sure I can believe a word that comes out of his mouth."

"Does he have a name?"

"Clay Stipes. Apparently, your uncle is familiar with him."

Veda said in outrage, "Clay Stipes the cop-killer? *He's* your source?"

"You see the trouble I have putting any faith in him?" His voice remained quietly controlled, but his expression was grim. "I get the impression he'd say or do anything for a payday. But on the slight chance he's telling the truth, I thought the details he provided might help jog your memory."

A rich, older man. *Oh, Lily. What did you get yourself into?*

Something flitted through Veda's head. Not exactly a memory but a faint nudge. There one moment and gone the next. She had no idea what it meant, but questions arose from the prompt. What if Jon was right? What if she knew more than she was willing to remember?

"What is it?" His tone rose slightly. "Do you know who he is?"

She shook her head. "No one fitting that description comes to mind. How did Stipes come by this information?"

"He's also an ex-cop. He claims he still has contacts in law enforcement."

"Then, why don't you just give him what he wants in exchange for a name?"

"It's complicated." He glanced over his shoulder as if worried Stipes might be within hearing distance. "An exchange of cash with a guy like Clay Stipes can result in unintended consequences. He's not someone I want to do business with, much less be indebted to."

"That's probably a wise decision," she agreed. "For the

sake of argument, let's say you somehow find Lily's mystery man on your own. What's your plan? Do you go knock on his door and accuse him of killing my sister and your brother without any evidence?"

Another faint smile. "I would hope to be a little more subtle. First, we find out his name, and then we look for the evidence."

"Uh-uh. There is no *we*." She was adamant. "I already told you I don't want any part of this."

"But what if you're the key to uncovering his identity?"

"And what if you're still grasping at straws?" she shot back.

That shut him down but only for a moment. "Think about it. Lily was eighteen and embroiled in a clandestine love affair. Forbidden love at that age can be very romantic, overwhelming even. Put yourself in her place. Would you be able to keep something like that a secret? You'd want to confide in someone close to you, someone you trusted."

Veda sighed. "How many times do I have to say it? She never told me his name."

"Maybe she told a best friend."

"It's been nearly two decades. I wouldn't even know where to find most of her friends. They all scattered years ago. And honestly, if she wouldn't tell me his name, I doubt she told anyone else."

"She may not have deliberately told you anything, but is it possible she let something slip? Maybe a nickname? Maybe his profession or where he lived?"

"If she did, I never caught on. She did say they were planning to go away together, but I already testified to that in court."

"Did she mention where they were going or when?"

"As I said on the stand, they hadn't yet worked out the details."

He paused again. "Do you think he could have been putting her off?"

"While still leading her on? That thought has crossed my mind."

"What about a journal or diary? She would have kept it hidden where no one would have come across it by accident. And what about mementos? Surely, she would have wanted keepsakes from the relationship? Photographs, love letters, *something*. If we could just sit down and talk things through… A few minutes of your time. That's all I'm asking. What have you got to lose?"

Her peace of mind, for one thing. Veda told herself to end it now. Just send him on his way and wash her hands of the whole mess. She was sorry for what he was going through, but nothing he had to say could change the fact that his brother had murdered her sister.

Even as the argument bubbled to her lips, though, an old doubt started to niggle.

He made no move toward her, nor she to him. They seemed to be in something of a standstill, each in their own way trapped in the past as their gazes locked. He looked pale and ghostlike in the fading light. Almost too handsome to be real with his dark, wavy hair falling over his forehead and those blue eyes so electric they could surely pierce her soul. His voice was a deep baritone with only a hint of a drawl. She could well imagine the effect that richness would have on a jury. It was certainly having an effect on her.

The situation was so strange, she thought. She and Jon Redmond standing face-to-face with twilight and honeysuckle weaving a cloak of mystery and nostalgia all around them.

She folded her arms and tried not to shiver. "You should go home." Her moment of weakness made her respond more sharply than she would have liked. "You should be with your family instead of standing here arguing with me."

"They're the reason I'm here," he said quietly. "They need to know the truth. It's all they have left."

"They have you. Go home, Jon. I can't help you."

"Can't or won't?"

"Both." Brushing past him, she climbed the porch steps without looking back. "It's been a long day, and I'm tired."

A car passed by on the street. He waited until the sound of the engine faded before he spoke. "Do you remember the last thing I said to you outside the courtroom that day?"

She slowly turned. "You said, 'My brother isn't a killer, and if it takes the rest of my life I'll find a way to prove it.'"

"Nothing has changed."

The depth of his conviction juxtaposed against the softness of his tone tore at her resolve. "You're conveniently dismissing the fact that your brother was convicted by a jury of his peers."

"A conviction that was overturned."

"For prosecutorial misconduct, not because he was innocent. His release on a legal technicality doesn't negate the fact that he was found with the murder weapon in his truck and my sister's blood all over his hands."

"You're dismissing something pretty damn important yourself. My brother was murdered, too. Less than twenty-four hours ago." He stared up at her from the bottom of the steps. "What if I'm right and Lily's killer is still out there?

What if he resurfaced years after her death to murder my brother?"

"Do you even hear yourself?" She came back over to the edge of the porch. "Why would Lily's killer come after Tony? If what you say is true, your brother was the scapegoat. Why cast doubt now on his guilt?"

"Whether you want to admit it or not, the overturned conviction has already cast doubt. Questions are being asked. Old memories are being stirred. I think Tony was murdered because of something he found out while he was still in prison. I think he knew the name of Lily's killer."

"You think, but you don't know. If it were true, why wouldn't he have told you?"

"I can't answer that."

"Can't or won't?" Veda moved back to the door and inserted the key.

"So that's it?" he said from behind her. "I just walk away, and that's the end of it?"

"What did you think was going to happen when you came over here? That I would throw up my hands and say *Go ahead, drag me into your delusion*?"

"It didn't go quite that way in my head."

She said in exasperation, "Why me?"

He answered without hesitation. "You knew Lily better than anyone. You have access to her belongings. You have a vested interest in finding out what really happened that night. And because you're the only Campion who would give me the time of day."

"The truth at last," she muttered as she turned back to the door. "I'm going inside to pour myself a very large glass of wine. It's been that kind of a day. If you're still here when I come back out, I'll give you five more minutes."

He was still at the bottom of the steps. "Thank you."

"Don't thank me yet. If I'm not convinced by the end of our talk, you have to walk away and leave me alone."

"Agreed."

She went inside and uncorked a bottle of wine. Then she went down the hallway to the bathroom to wash her face and straighten her ponytail. She refused to do any primping beyond that. No shower, no makeup, no change of clothing. She didn't need to impress Jon Redmond. The opposite, in fact. She needed to convince him once and for all that he was barking up the wrong Campion.

Returning to the kitchen, she poured a wineglass nearly to the brim, taking a quick sip to make sure none of the merlot spilled over. Then she poured a generous splash of bourbon into another glass and carried both drinks out to the porch.

Jon was seated on her porch swing by this time. He started to get up, but she waved him back down before placing the bourbon on the table in front of the swing. "You look like you could use this."

He picked up the glass. "Thanks, but I'm coasting on fumes as it is. If I drink this, I may fall asleep right here on your porch." He sipped tentatively.

She looked him over. "How long has it been since you slept?"

"I've lost track. Night before last, I think."

She sat down in a chair across from the swing and drank generously. "You look like hell."

"So you've mentioned. Although I believe *death warmed-over* was your previous assessment."

She propped her feet on a wicker ottoman and continued to drink. He did not. The silence that ensued was hardly companionable, yet for some reason, Veda wasn't compelled to hurry him along. Maybe it was those damning circles beneath his eyes or the furrows of grief and worry across his brow. She knew only too well what he was going through. His haunted blue eyes stirred a myriad of emotions. Try as she might to remain hard-hearted or at least wary, she felt her determination slip with each passing moment.

He set the rest of his drink on the table, then leaned back against the swing. "This is a nice place."

"It's a short-term rental. I don't know how long I'll be in town. I never thought I'd be here this long."

"Plans change," he said. "I never thought I'd be a lawyer."

The confession surprised her. She said over the rim of her wineglass, "No? I hear you're pretty good at it."

The swing rocked gently. The motion seemed to hypnotize him. "I wanted to be an architect like my grandfather. Design and build beautiful houses. *Forever homes*, he called them."

Veda idly twirled her ponytail around one finger. "It's never too late."

"Yeah, it is. I made my decision a long time ago. After Tony's conviction, I knew what I had to do. He went to prison, and I went back to school and changed my major to pre-law."

"Never looked back?"

"I wouldn't say never, but not often." He eyed the bourbon but didn't pick up the glass. "What about you? Why pathology?"

She said a little defensively, "Why not pathology? You're not the squeamish type, are you?"

He gave a humorless laugh. "Not anymore. I only asked

because I was curious if what happened to Lily had anything to do with your career choice."

Veda shrugged. "Maybe a little. I always knew I wanted a career in medicine. During my junior and senior years, I worked for Dr. Bader after school and on summer break. Mostly clerical work at first, but once I turned eighteen, he allowed me to observe some of the procedures. It took some getting used to."

Jon grimaced. "I'm sure."

She smiled at his tone. "But you do get used to it after a while. And you learn not to eat certain things before certain procedures. Eventually, I realized that working at the morgue wasn't so different from working in a hospital. A surgeon operates to save a life. A pathologist operates to find out why the person died. And in some cases, we're able to uncover clues along the way as to the who, what, when and where. It's important work."

"Not just important but integral to the criminal justice system," he agreed. "What happens in the autopsy room can free the innocent or send the guilty to jail. Unfortunately, the opposite is sometimes true."

She acknowledged his point with a nod as she studied him in the deepening twilight. She couldn't get over his appearance. Not the disheveled hair or rumpled clothing, but the blue eyes and the chiseled jawline. She supposed he'd always been attractive, but she couldn't remember noticing. Now she'd have a hard time forgetting. Never again would she think of Jon Redmond as anyone's big brother. He was his own man, and somewhere along the way he'd grown exceedingly handsome.

"What's wrong?"

She shrugged and sipped her wine. "I was thinking

about our conversation at the cemetery. You made a point of letting me know that Dr. Bader overextends himself and cuts corners, yet I got the impression you were worried about more than his competence. When I mentioned kickbacks, you hesitated before you admitted you didn't have any proof."

He said carefully, "You know why my brother's conviction was overturned, right?"

"Yes, the DA supposedly withheld evidence from the defense."

Jon's eyes flashed in the dusk. "Not supposedly. He did. Two key pieces of exculpatory evidence. Or at the very least, evidence that could have been used by Tony's defense team to create reasonable doubt." He took a breath, seemingly to get his anger under control. "Do you remember the results of Lily's tox screen?"

"Of course. The lab found traces of benzodiazepine in her blood. The DA argued that Tony used Rohypnol to impair her senses so she couldn't fight back."

"Did you know that my brother was also given a blood test?"

She was caught off guard by the question but tried not to show it. "I'm not surprised. It would have been standard operating procedure. Dr. Bader likely collected the sample himself."

"He did. The lab sent back two reports. The preliminary analysis checked for alcohol, prescription and nonprescription medicines, illegal drugs like marijuana, cocaine, heroin, that type of thing. The second, more in-depth analysis turned up the same benzodiazepine found in Lily's blood. That finding was never turned over to the defense, much less presented to the jury."

Veda frowned. "How would that even be possible? Too many people would have known about the second report."

"How many of them followed the trial that closely? The state crime lab is notoriously backlogged. Once they turn over their findings, they move on to the next case unless called to testify."

She came right back at him. "Even if what you're saying is true, the presence of benzodiazepine in Tony's blood test wouldn't have cleared him of murder. He could have dosed himself to numb his senses. Date-rape drugs aren't just used to spike drinks. They're sometimes used recreationally."

"Rarely," Jon argued. "They're considered minor euphoriants at best. But the bigger point is this." He leaned forward. "After the murder, Tony supposedly drove all the way across town to find a railroad crossing. The amount of benzodiazepine in his system would have made that virtually impossible." Then, as if to hammer home his point, he added, "There was also a witness."

She said in shock, "To the murder?"

"Not to the murder, no. A witness saw someone exit Tony's truck and run off into the woods. The witness thought at first the vehicle had stalled on the tracks and the driver had gone for help. He didn't have a working phone so he also went for help. By the time he returned, the truck had been pushed from the tracks and Tony was lying cuffed on the ground surrounded by police."

"Why didn't this person check the vehicle to make sure no one else was inside before he left?"

"He assumed any passengers would have gotten out, too."

"Could he identify the person who ran into the woods?"

"It was too dark, and he was too far away."

Veda shook her head. "Sorry, but his story sounds a little fishy to me. Why did this witness never come forward?"

"He did, but as you can imagine, the scene was chaotic that night. By the time he came back, the police had found the knife in Tony's truck, and they were desperately trying to ascertain where all that blood on his hands and clothing came from. The witness reported what he saw to an officer at the scene, but he was never called in to give a formal statement, much less to testify."

"Then, how did you find out about him?"

"An office assistant who used to work in the DA's office finally came forward. She swore in her deposition that the officer's notes and the second tox screen were originally included in Tony's file. They went missing sometime before his case went to trial."

"Let me guess. Is this assistant a disgruntled former employee?"

"More like someone with a guilty conscience and enough foresight to make duplicates of everything in order to protect herself from a corrupt prosecutor who would have thought nothing of trumping up charges to ruin her life if she tried to go public with the information."

"So why come forward now?" Veda pressed.

"Her former boss has retired from politics. Allegations of corruption, go figure. He doesn't have the power or clout he once hoped to have in this state. But as to the real reason for her timing, only she knows for sure. I would hope that her sense of justice prevailed. What I know is that my brother was denied a fair trial. The DA deliberately withheld those two pieces of evidence because he knew a conviction would help advance his career. It wouldn't be the first time."

"And Dr. Bader? Where does he fit in?"

"The lab would have sent Tony's toxicology report to his office, and he would have made a copy for the police department. At the very least, there was willful negligence on the part of the coroner's office and/or the police department. I have a theory as to why."

"I'm all ears," she said.

He gave her a look she couldn't decipher. "Cops can be notoriously single-minded when they think they have a suspect dead to rights. They found the murder weapon in Tony's truck. Lily's blood was all over his hands and clothing. And he was in what they called an *unresponsive state*. Any piece of evidence that didn't corroborate their case against him could have been easily discounted or ignored."

"You're painting with an awfully broad brush," she accused.

"I don't think so. Not considering the outcome. The tox screen and the eyewitness account along with your testimony about a secret boyfriend could have been used by the defense to create reasonable doubt. Without the other two pieces of evidence, the DA was able to use your testimony to prove motive."

"All I did was tell the truth."

"I know." He turned to glance out over the small front yard, his expression enigmatic. She followed his gaze and wondered if he'd spotted the lone lightning bug she'd seen earlier in the boxwoods. Or maybe he'd drifted back in time before her sister's murder had jaded and changed them all.

And maybe it was time to call it a night and send him on his way. He'd made a good case, but she wasn't yet ready to concede aloud her doubts. His brother had been the bad guy in her head for too many years. She wasn't going to change her mind overnight no matter how persuasive she found his argument.

And yet...

"Tell me about Lily."

She'd been so deep in thought that the request startled her. She shook off her reverie. "What do you want to know?"

"Whatever you want me to know." He watched her from the swing, his eyes blinking drowsily, but the color, even in twilight, was still amazingly vivid. "I didn't know her all that well. Which seems strange, in hindsight. She and Tony were inseparable for years."

"Sometimes I wonder how well I knew her," Veda admitted. "She was smart. Beautiful. Complicated. She could be funny at times but also moody and too often depressed. And secretive. But you already know that. She was also deathly afraid of thunderstorms."

"Why was she afraid of storms?"

"The car wreck that killed our dad happened during a storm. He and Lily were very close. Don't get me wrong. He loved all of us kids. He was a great dad. But even as a child, Lily had this aura about her, this otherworldly beauty that caused people to stop on the street and stare at her. Sometimes they'd even ask my mom if they could take her picture. I think my dad was so protective because he knew her kind of beauty might someday attract the wrong kind of attention."

"In that case, he must have been protective of you, too."

She felt inordinately flattered by the insinuation. Had it been that long since a man had paid her a compliment? Or maybe she was just a little bit tipsy. One very full glass of wine had lowered her defenses.

"I wasn't in Lily's league, and I was okay with that,"

she said. "This may sound phony and a little too self-aggrandizing, but I never felt jealous of all the attention. Living in her shadow gave me a certain amount of freedom."

"That's a very healthy way of dealing with sibling rivalry. I wasn't that mature. I envied Tony's talent. He didn't just excel at football, he broke records. I was a mediocre baseball player at best." But despite his deprecating tone, he didn't come off as bitter or resentful. He sounded proud. "Did you know he had a full-ride scholarship to Ole Miss? Those aren't easy to come by. He could have ended up in the pros, he was that good. Someone took all that away from him. I want to know why."

Veda's eyes stung unexpectedly. "Someone stole Lily's future, too. Do you really think finding her mystery man is going to give you the answers you need?"

"I think he's a good place to start. One real lead is all we need."

She sighed. "You expect a lot. What makes you think we can undercover something that no one else has been able to do in seventeen years?"

"Because no one else has been looking."

"You have."

"I was more focused on getting my brother out of prison."

"Still…" She gazed down into her empty glass. "I don't think you should get your hopes up."

"I was told the same thing about every stage of the appeal."

"This is different," Veda insisted. "You think Lily left something behind—a photo or a journal or a letter that will give you a clue. She didn't. The police searched her room after the murder. I've been through her things myself. Nothing is there. But—"

"But?" His tone was hopeful.

"I'll take another look just to put your mind at ease."

"Thank you."

Veda decided she must really be feeling no pain to make such an offer. She glanced at his glass on the table. Except for an initial sip or two, he hadn't touched his drink. "It's getting late."

"Yes, you're right. I've worn out my welcome and then some." He stood, and she walked him to the edge of the porch. He caught her arm when she teetered on the top step. "You okay?"

"Just tired."

Dusk had fallen in earnest, and the streetlights were on. The moths had come out to bask in the glow, and the bats had come out to feast.

Jon was still holding onto her arm. "Get some rest. We can talk again if you want. If not...thanks for hearing me out."

Before she could duck or even catch her breath, he bent and kissed her cheek. Far from being repelled, she had the strongest urge to turn her head to meet his lips.

Chapter Seven

Jon was half-dead on his feet as he climbed the outside steps to his apartment. He automatically checked his surroundings as he removed his key from his pocket. The day's events had left him both exhausted and wary. His brother had been murdered less than twenty-four hours ago. He kept waiting for that reality to sink in, but at the moment he mostly felt numb.

He'd grieved for Tony when the verdict had been read aloud in the courtroom and every time thereafter when he'd visited the prison or an appeal had hit a brick wall. He hated to acknowledge that in a very real sense, he'd said goodbye to his brother a long time ago.

His phone pinged with an incoming text message. He checked the screen. Gabby, wanting to know when he was coming back. He thumbed a response: Grabbing a quick shower and change of clothing at the apartment. Be back in a few.

Gabby: You've been gone a long time. Mom's worried.

Jon: Tell her I'm fine. I'll be there soon. Love you both.

His sister's texts momentarily distracted him. The last

thing he wanted was to worry his mother, but there were things that required his attention. Still, he needed to be more mindful of his family's needs. To that end, he'd pack a bag while he was at the apartment so that he wouldn't have to come back for a couple of days. He planned to spend the next few nights with his mom and Gabby, not just as a safety precaution but because in his experience, the absence of a loved one was more keenly felt after dark.

His steps slowed as he approached his apartment. The door was ajar. He checked over his shoulder before nudging it open with his foot. The hinges swung silently inward. He'd turned off all the lights when he left early that morning, but enough illumination streamed in through the balcony windows to allow him a view down the narrow foyer and into the living room. No movement. No sound. Everything was silent inside.

Bending to check the doorjamb, he traced his finger across scratches in the wood that could have been made by a jimmy. Then he rose and stepped across the threshold, his gaze darting from one dim corner to the next. Satisfied that he was alone, he closed the door with a soft click. The sound sent a warning chill up his spine, and he paused yet again to listen. The only noise he could detect was the rev of an engine down in the parking lot. Nothing came to him from the depths of the apartment.

Even so, he knew better than to let his guard down. His brother had just been murdered, and now his apartment had been broken into. A connection seemed like a distinct possibility. He wouldn't put it past Clay Stipes to break in looking for money or as a means to coerce and intimidate him.

A vision formed in his head of Tony on his knees, hands bound behind his back. Jon's heart tripped in trepidation.

The safest move was to leave the apartment and call the police from his vehicle. Instead, he held his ground, tuning his senses to the slightest movement or noise.

At first glance, nothing seemed out of place. Maybe the intruder had been caught in the act or gotten cold feet. He was probably long gone by now. As Jon's eyes adjusted to the dark, he noticed one of the drawers in the TV credenza had been left open. A seemingly innocuous detail that on any other day he could have easily blamed on his carelessness. Now he knew with certainty that someone had been in his apartment looking for something.

He moved back to the foyer, extracting a baseball bat from the coat closet. His fingers tightened around the grip as he moved across the living room and down the hallway to his office. He peeked in through the open doorway before stepping inside. The desk drawers were closed, and his laptop and tablet didn't appear to have been touched. Strange, because small electronics would be easy pickings for someone wanting to make a quick buck. But he had a feeling the intruder had been after something else.

Still hovering just inside, he turned to move into the hallway when he caught a slight movement from the corner of his eye. He whirled a split second before the door slammed into him, hitting him in the face and knocking him back into the hallway. His head hit the wall with a thud. Before he could shake off the daze, the door flew back and a shadow sprang from his office.

The intruder body-slammed him against the wall, and Jon went sprawling to the floor even as he swung the bat. He connected with a shin bone. He heard a grunt, and then the attacker lunged. Jon lifted the bat in both hands to deflect the heavy metal flashlight that slashed through the dark toward his head. The casing struck the bat, shattering the lens. Glass shards rained down, piercing him above the left eyebrow.

Blood ran down into his eye, but he didn't have time to wipe it away. He was on his back on the floor, the assailant looming over him. Tossing the flashlight aside, the attacker grabbed the bat with both hands and forced it down against Jon's windpipe. He pushed back hard, but the man was strong and in the position of power, using his body weight for leverage. Jon tried to take in details of his appearance, but it was dark in the hallway and the intruder was dressed all in black. He could have been Stipes; he could have been anyone. They grappled for what seemed an eternity until the man wrested the bat free from Jon's grip. Then he lifted it over his head and swung hard. Jon jerked to the side, dodging a skull-crushing blow, but the bat caught his right temple hard enough to stun him.

He fought his way up through the haze as he braced for a fresh attack. None came. A moment later, he heard the door of his apartment slam shut.

A FULL THIRTY minutes went by before the police arrived. During the interim, Jon called his sister to say that he would be a little longer than expected. Everything was fine, but he had to take care of some business. He'd tell them the real reason for the delay soon enough, but now was not the time to distress his family any more than they already were.

Two uniforms finally showed up at his door. They asked Jon to accompany them through the apartment, checking the contents of drawers and his desk to see what, if anything, was missing. They took pictures with their phones and dusted the flat surfaces and doorknobs for prints.

While they worked, Jon sat on the couch with an ice pack to his right temple and a washcloth pressed to the cut over his left brow to stanch the blood. He felt annoyed, unsettled and mildly embarrassed to have had his own baseball bat used against him. At least he was alive. All things considered he accounted himself respectably if not spectacularly, but this wasn't about ego. This was about turf. Someone had broken into his home and gone through his belongings. If he found out Clay Stipes was behind the intrusion—

The sound of the door buzzer interrupted his misery. He put the ice pack and washcloth aside and got up, glancing down the hallway toward his office as he moved to the door. Marcus Campion stood on the other side. He had his back to Jon as he gazed down at the parking lot.

Jon said in surprise, "Marcus. What are you doing here?"

The police chief turned with a scowl. "I heard you had some trouble here tonight."

"Someone broke in." Jon gestured toward the tool marks on the doorjamb.

Marcus gave the damage a cursory glance, then gazed past Jon into the apartment. "Okay if I come in and have a look around?"

"Sure, but the officers that responded have already taken my statement. They're just down the hall in my office dusting for prints." He stepped aside to allow the chief to enter.

He was out of uniform as he had been at the cemetery, but he'd taken the time to strap on a holster and clip his badge to his belt. His sleeves were rolled up, displaying powerful forearms, and he walked into the apartment with his shoulders thrown back and his head held high, making the most of his six-foot-plus frame. The guy appeared to be in excellent shape for his age, but Jon's admiration ended with his fitness.

He didn't have much use for Marcus Campion as a police chief or as a human being. He remembered only too well the way Marcus had treated his family after Tony's arrest. He hadn't been the police chief back then nor had he been assigned to the case as a detective. However, he'd managed to insinuate himself into the investigation at every turn. Back then, Jon had thought him arrogant, surly and a bully. His opinion had only strengthened since his time as the Webber County DA. They'd managed to hammer out a working relationship, but anytime he was in the police chief's presence, he always sensed a power struggle simmering beneath the surface.

"You seem nervous," Marcus observed.

"Not nervous, just surprised. A B and E seems a few notches below your pay grade."

"The brother of my murder victim has his apartment broken into less than twenty-four hours later, that catches my attention."

Jon was quick to latch onto the observation. "You think there's a connection?"

"You tell me." Marcus stood just inside the doorway, feet slightly apart as his gaze moved slowly around the living room. Then his focus came back to Jon, and his eyes narrowed. "You don't look so good."

"That seems to be the consensus," he muttered.

Marcus gave a nod to the cut above his brow. "Did he do that?"

"Sort of. He tried to clock me with a flashlight. The lens broke, and a piece of glass sliced me."

"Damn. You're still oozing blood there, bud. You should probably get that stitched up."

"I'm fine," he lied. He was starting to feel a little woozy, and the last thing he wanted was to collapse, literally, at Marcus Campion's feet. He moved back into the living room and sat down, giving a laconic wave toward the hallway. "Your officers are down that way."

"I'll just be a minute. Don't go anywhere," Marcus added before he disappeared down the hallway. Jon heard him conversing with the officers, but he couldn't make out what they were saying.

Having Marcus Campion show up at his door was almost as unnerving as the break-in. Garrett Calloway was the lead detective. He should be the one investigating a connection to Tony's murder, but Jon couldn't say he was surprised by the turn of events. He'd suspected all along that Marcus would be running things behind the scene.

He pressed the washcloth to his brow and then lifted the ice pack to his pounding temple. Nausea still roiled a little too close to the surface. He lay his head back against the couch and closed his eyes. Not a good day by any measure. All he'd wanted was a few minutes alone to clean up and maybe have a little time to mourn his brother in peace. Instead, here he sat with blood trickling down his face, an ice pack to his head and an apartment full of cops.

The one bright spot, if he could be so optimistic, was the time he'd spent with Veda. Maybe it was wishful thinking, but she seemed to be coming around to the notion of his brother's innocence. At the very least, he had her thinking. From everything he knew about her professional reputation, she was capable and conscientious and had a keen sense of justice. Whether she'd ultimately decide to help him remained to be seen, but she'd promised to have another look through Lily's things, and at the moment that was really all he could ask for.

Maybe she was right. Maybe it was foolish to think that a clue could still turn up after all this time. The police had searched Lily's room after the murder, and the family had undoubtedly packed away or gotten rid of most of her personal belongings a long time ago. Nothing *should* be there, but Jon's gut told him otherwise. A young woman entangled in a forbidden love affair would want to keep something from her lover close by.

If all else failed, he could still strike a bargain with Clay Stipes, but he had a feeling that would be akin to selling his soul to the devil. Once money exchanged hands, Stipes could claim anything he damn well pleased to try and extract more. A made-up murder-for-hire scheme might be the least of it.

His thoughts continued to ramble until Marcus came back out to the living room and sat down across from him. He didn't take notes or ask questions, just sat staring at Jon for a few seconds, probably trying to intimidate him.

Jon didn't take the bait. He placed the ice pack on the coffee table with careless disregard for the surface. Then he removed the washcloth from his cut and examined the smears of blood. The little tasks were unhurried because he didn't want to leave the impression with Marcus Campion that he could be rattled.

When Marcus finally spoke, his voice was devoid of even the slightest hint of concern, let alone sympathy. "Hasn't been a very good day for you, has it, Jon?"

"Not one of my better ones," he agreed.

"Sounds like you put up a fight, so there's that." He almost sounded impressed.

Jon shrugged. "Not much of a consolation in my book. Were the officers able to lift any prints?"

"A few, but I doubt they belong to the perp. We'll need a set of yours for comparison." He drummed his fingertips on the arm of the chair as his gaze roamed the space. "Walk me through what happened."

Jon recounted the moments when he'd first arrived home to discover the front door ajar and the tool marks on the doorjamb. Then entering the apartment, he'd noticed the open drawer in the credenza before moving down the hallway to his office.

"Until then, I had no idea he was still in the apartment," Jon said. "He must have been hiding behind the door when I looked inside the office."

"You didn't recognize him?"

"I never got a good look at him. He knocked me back into the hallway with the door. Next thing I knew, I was on the floor fighting for my life."

"You must have noticed something," Marcus pressed.

"I wish I had, but the hallway was dark. I think he closed the blinds in the office to block out the streetlights. Now that I think back, he may have been wearing something over his face."

"Like a mask?"

Jon frowned in concentration. "A ski mask or a hoodie. I can't say for sure."

"What about his height, his build? Tall, short, fat, skinny…"

He shrugged again. "Like I said, it was dark, and it happened fast. I would say he was about my height. Not fat, not thin. Average, I guess. He was strong, though."

"What about distinguishing marks? Tattoos, scars, birth marks."

"Again, it was dark, and he was dressed in black. I've already gone over this with the responding officers."

"Humor me."

"We were on the floor most of the time. I won't bother giving you a blow-by-blow account, but once he got his hands on the baseball bat, he swung for my skull." Jon pointed to the bump at the side of his head.

"Did you lose consciousness?"

"No, but I was dazed. All I remember afterward was the sound of the front door slamming shut."

"You didn't try to pursue?"

"It took me a minute to get to my feet."

"You've got some blood…" Marcus made an up and down motion with his finger.

Jon grabbed the washcloth and wiped away a fresh trail of blood.

"Are you sure you don't want to go to the ER?"

He was less sure by the moment. "Head injuries always bleed a lot."

"It's your funeral." Marcus leaned in, resting his forearms on his thighs. "Here's my take. The guy was a pro. He had the right tool to get inside the apartment without making too much noise or taking too much time. He went for the drawers and left the electronics." He nodded toward the flat-screen mounted on the wall. "TVs with those kinds of mounts take too long and too much effort, plus he'd then have to carry it down the stairs and out to his vehicle. But your laptop and tablet were in plain sight on your desk.

He didn't touch them, either. I'll be honest with you. The prints we found are likely yours. He wouldn't have been that careless."

Jon still had the washcloth pressed to his head. "What about a connection to my brother's murder?"

"Still a possibility. Not much to go on, but I'm not a big believer in coincidences. As of now, though, we'll investigate each crime separately unless and until we can connect them."

Jon gave a vague nod. "Anything new on Tony's case?"

"Since you called Detective Calloway this afternoon? Yeah, that's right. He mentioned he'd already heard from you. Give the man a chance to do his job. It hasn't even been twenty-four hours."

Jon pressed on. "What about ballistics?"

Marcus sighed. "As of yet, no matches. Whoever killed your brother was smart enough to use a clean gun. No fingerprints at the murder scene, no way to distinguish footprints and tire tracks from dozens of others. He knew what he was doing. Just like this guy."

"Dr. Bader said the plastic strap used to restrain Tony's wrists could have been a zip tie." Jon paused, trying not to dwell on the images flashing through his head. His brother on his knees, a gun to his head. "Probably the heavy-duty kind used by law enforcement," he added.

Marcus lifted a brow. "You mean the kind that any DIYer can pick up at a local hardware store?" His eyes flashed a warning. "Remember what I said earlier about throwing around unfounded accusations."

"It was an observation, not an accusation."

"For now, let's just stick to the break-in," Marcus said. "Although, your observations about the assailant haven't been very helpful so far. Assuming the cases are unrelated, is there any reason someone might think you'd have a large amount of cash stashed in here? He could have been watching your place for a couple of days. Have you been to the bank or an ATM recently?"

"Not in the past few days."

"You haven't taken out a cash loan, have you?"

The question caught Jon off guard, though he tried not to show it. Had Marcus Campion somehow found out about his missed appointment at the bank that morning?

"No loans," he said. "No recent withdrawals. I don't flash money around in public. I don't know why someone would think I'd leave cash lying around the apartment."

"Then, maybe he was looking for information," Marcus suggested. "Maybe the break-in has something to do with one of your cases. I saw a bunch of files back in your office."

"It's possible," Jon conceded. "But anything in those folders is already public knowledge. I don't keep sensitive casefiles in my apartment."

Marcus was silent for a moment, but his focus remained on Jon. "Have you heard from Clay Stipes since we talked this morning?"

"I'm hoping he left town."

"That doesn't exactly answer my question. I can't help but wonder about his timing. He showed up in town right after Tony got out of prison. What do you think they were up to?"

Jon was immediately defensive. "What makes you think they were up to something?"

"Both convicted felons. One a cop-killer. Don't tell me they weren't planning something."

Jon took a quick breath and swallowed past the cold anger that had been building since Marcus Campion's phone call early that morning. Now was not the time to antagonize the local police chief, let alone reveal a thirst for revenge.

"My brother wasn't a criminal. He was unjustly charged by a corrupt prosecutor who deliberately withheld evidence from the defense and the jury in order to put another notch in his belt."

Marcus scoffed. "And I suppose the murder weapon just magically appeared in the back of Tony's truck?"

"It was planted, probably by the man who was seen running away from the railroad tracks."

"You mean the man who conveniently came forward when he needed the services of a hotshot law firm to help him beat a third-offense DUI charge? That man?"

"He wasn't compensated for his disposition, if that's what you're trying to imply. He also came forward originally. He told an officer at the scene what he saw, but for some strange reason, he was never called in to give a formal statement. The officer's notes ended up in a file along with a copy of Tony's toxicology screen that showed traces of the same drug found in Lily's blood. Yet both pieces of evidence went missing before the trial."

"What can I tell you? Things happen."

His smirky indifference infuriated Jon despite his best efforts to remain calm. "Did you know about that witness?"

"I didn't much like that question the first time you asked it. But my answer is still the same."

Jon wasn't to be deterred. "Did you know my brother was dosed with benzodiazepine? Tell me you wouldn't let an innocent kid rot in prison because you needed someone to take the blame for Lily's murder."

"Innocent kid." He all but spat the words as he lifted a finger and jabbed it in Jon's direction. "Now, you listen to me, you little—" He broke off as the officers came down the hallway and into the living room. "What is it?"

They kept their distance, either out of reverence, fear or an intense dislike of Marcus Campion. "We're heading back to the station unless you need something else."

Something else? Jon couldn't help but wonder what they'd already done for the man.

"Wait outside," Marcus barked. "I'll be down in a minute."

As soon as the door closed behind them, he jumped to his feet so that he could look down at Jon. "That investigation was conducted by the book. No one needed to withhold anything. The evidence was overwhelming. We had a body, we had a murder weapon, and we had a jilted boyfriend covered in my niece's blood."

"And I have a dead brother." Jon rose slowly. "I'm putting you on notice. If you or anyone in your department try to hide evidence or back-burner this investigation, I'll be coming for you."

Marcus's mouth thinned as his gaze hardened. "You may be the DA—for now—but no one is above the law. If you interfere in an official investigation, I'll have no choice but to have you arrested."

"The district attorney's office has every right to conduct an independent investigation if we deem the local police incapable, unwilling or unfit."

"Do you think that scares me?" Marcus shrugged. "Go ahead. Conduct whatever investigation you like, but you better brace yourself. You might not like what you find."

"I'll take my chances. All I care about is the truth."

Marcus gave him a knowing look. "Sure. Keep telling yourself that."

"What's that supposed to mean?"

"Admit it, Jon. You don't care about the truth. You just want your pound of flesh. You blame me and my family for what happened to your family, but it wasn't a Campion who put a knife in Tony's hand that night. And it wasn't a Campion who shot him in the back of the head."

"You don't know that."

"I know this. You keep harassing my niece, I'll be the one coming for you."

That stopped Jon cold. "*Harassing?* Did she say that?"

"She didn't have to. She feels about you the same way the rest of us do, so I know she didn't seek you out. You accosted her at the cemetery this morning, and your car was spotted at her house earlier this evening. You're not going to deny it, are you?"

Jon's anger flared. "You son of a bitch. Are you having me followed?"

Marcus gave him a tight smile. "I'm keeping an eye on a lot of things. Remember this while you conduct your *independent* investigation. You may be the DA, but this is my town. I take care of my own."

Chapter Eight

The next morning, Veda received a call from her mother inviting her to lunch. Since they'd spent so much time together the day before, not all of it pleasant, she started to beg off. But then she felt guilty and accepted. Between the heart attack and Tony Redmond's release from prison—and now his murder—her mom was having a hard time. She spent too much time alone in that big house with too many painful memories. Wasn't that why Veda had returned to her hometown in the first place? To reconnect with her family and offer moral support when needed? It also didn't hurt that the lunch invitation gave her an opportunity to search through Lily's belongings.

Owen's truck and Nate's SUV were parked in the drive when she got there. She hadn't known beforehand that her brothers were also coming to lunch, and their presence complicated things. They were both observant and nosy and would undoubtedly have questions if she spent too much time in Lily's room. Not that she was doing anything wrong, but she really didn't want to have to explain herself. She could only imagine what they would say if they found out she'd agreed to help Jon Redmond.

She let herself in the front door and called to her mom.

When she didn't get a response, she went through to the kitchen and glanced out the back door. Owen reclined on the patio with a beer while Nate manned the grill, fanning aside thick clouds of smoke that swirled up from the charcoals. When she opened the door to say hello, the scent of mesquite wafted into the kitchen.

Her mother came in carrying an assortment of roses and irises she'd picked from the garden.

"I didn't know the boys would be here," Veda commented.

"Nate offered to grill when he heard you were coming over. He called Owen, and here we all are."

"Don't they both have work today?"

Her mother was busy clipping flower stems at the sink. "Nate has the day off, and Owen is between projects. He's been promising to trim the hedges for weeks, so today seemed as good a time as any." She placed the flowers in a crystal vase, then stood back to admire her handiwork. "What do you think?"

"Absolutely beautiful," Veda said. "And the roses smell divine."

"Don't they? Nothing makes me happier than fresh flowers in the house." Despite her mother's bright tone, she still looked pale and a little careworn as if she hadn't gotten much sleep the night before. Veda couldn't help noticing the dark smudges beneath her eyes and the worry lines across her brow.

"Are you feeling okay, Mom?"

"What?" She seemed momentarily distracted. "Yes, I'm fine. Just a little tired."

"Still not sleeping well?"

"I managed to get a few hours last night. Stop worrying about me, Veda. I'm taking good care of myself, I promise.

I'm eating healthily, I walk every morning, and my blood pressure is normal. Everything is fine."

Except for the fact that she couldn't sleep, but Veda decided to let the matter drop. "What can I do to help?" she asked briskly. "Nate seems to have the grill well in hand."

Her mom passed her a basket. "You can run out to the garden and pick some fresh tomatoes while I rinse the lettuce for the salad."

"I have a better idea. Why don't you sit down and rest while I take care of the salad? I'll make some iced tea, too."

"What did I just say about fussing over me?" Her mom got out the chopping board. "The tea is already made, and I like keeping busy. Now, leave me alone, and go pick my tomatoes."

Veda had always enjoyed working in the garden. She took her time with the tomatoes, promising herself she would come over more often to help with the chores. But she needed to ease up a bit. She could keep an eye on her mom's mental and physical well-being without trying to overcompensate for all the years she'd been away.

A little while later they sat down to an informal lunch at the breakfast table. It was the first time the family had shared an impromptu weekday meal since Veda had returned home. She couldn't help noticing how they all avoided the subject of Tony Redmond. His release from prison had been the topic of conversation for weeks, but now that he was dead, it almost seemed as if his name had become taboo. She wanted to ask Owen if he'd heard from the police, but now was not the time. Besides, if any new developments arose, Nate would surely keep her informed.

She sipped iced tea as her gaze went around the table. Nate, stoic and silent. Owen, careless and confident. Their mom, chatty but with an edge of something that might have been despair below the surface. Tony's release and subsequent murder had stirred a lot of memories, so much so that Lily was almost a presence at the table. Veda wondered again what her family would say if they knew about her conversations with Jon Redmond. They wouldn't like her spending time with him no matter the reason. They might even feel betrayed. Any quarter given to the enemy could drive a wedge through the fragile bond she'd tried to forge with her brothers since her return. But guilt niggled. In trying to uncover Lily's secrets she was now keeping one of her own.

After lunch Nate, not Veda, insisted their mother lie down and rest for a bit. Surprisingly, she didn't argue with her eldest as she had with Veda. Instead, she seemed only too happy to escape to her room for an afternoon respite. Veda loaded the dishwasher and cleaned up the kitchen while Nate went out to cut the grass and Owen tackled the overgrown hedges. As soon as she heard the lawn mower engine, she left the kitchen and went upstairs to Lily's bedroom.

She started with the dresser and methodically searched through the drawers before moving to the plastic bins in the closet. She'd already looked through most of the storage containers the day before, but she made herself go through them again just in case. Satisfied that she hadn't missed anything, she put everything back where she found it and then glanced around the bedroom in contemplation. No obvious hiding place that she could discern. She even checked for loose floorboards and behind the artwork.

The drone of the mower in the backyard drifted up to her. The sound was somnolent in the afternoon heat. She lay down on the bed and stared at the ceiling as memories stirred. She thought about the dream her sister had shared on the night of her eighteenth birthday. The image of someone coming through Lily's window during a storm had been terrifying at the time, but now Veda could easily discern the symbolism. Lily's guilt—not the thunder—had summoned the bad man.

The demonic red eyes, the smell… Veda shivered as she tried to further intuit the meaning. The scent of cedar seemed both incongruous and innocuous, though she vaguely recalled a spiritual significance to the fragrance. But not just cedar. Specifically, the scent of their grandmother's old cedar chest.

Veda hadn't seen that piece in years. Mementos from her grandfather's time in the military had been stored inside, and her grandmother had kept the chest at the foot of her bed. When Veda was a kid, she hadn't given much thought to the placement, only that she'd loved going through all the photos and metals inside. Now she understood. Her grandmother had kept the piece close to her bed because she wanted to be near her beloved husband's keepsakes while she slept.

After her grandmother passed away and her house had been cleared out, Veda's mom had had Nate and Owen haul the chest up to the attic, along with a few other sentimental items she wanted to keep.

Veda bolted upright. Why would Lily's subconscious manifest the distinct scent of their grandmother's cedar chest and associate it with the bad man? Why…unless the cedar chest had been on her mind before she fell asleep that night?

Swinging her legs over the side of the bed, Veda got up

and went over to the window to glance down into the backyard. The sound of the mower was more distant now that Nate had moved around to the front. Her brothers would be finishing the yard work soon. She'd have a quick look through the attic and then go back downstairs to wait for them.

She left Lily's room and went to the top of the stairs. The house below was silent. She felt a little foolish going to such lengths to conceal her task, but Tony Redmond had been the literal bad man in her family for so long that she had a hard time justifying her actions even to herself. Nothing would probably come of the search anyway. *Just get it over with and move on.*

Rather than the pull-down ladders found in more modern houses, the attic access was a real staircase hidden behind a latched door. Veda peered up the narrow steps as she recalled the time she'd been locked inside. While she'd waited for someone to come and let her out, her imagination had played cruel tricks. She'd been convinced that the ghosts of previous owners lurked in all the shadowy corners. She'd worked herself into such a state that she'd been willing to risk life and limb by climbing out a window.

More than two decades had passed, and yet she still held a grudge against her brothers for pulling that stunt. She'd never believed the faulty-latch excuse, but she left the door ajar just in case.

The stairwell was unlit, but enough sunlight spilled in through the double windows to guide her up the steps. The space was typical of a hundred-year-old house: creaky floorboards, dusty windows and every inch of space beneath the slanted roofline stacked with boxes, lamps, sporting equipment and the odd piece of furniture.

She had to do some digging and rearranging to get to the cedar chest. Pulling it out into the sunlight, she tried the clasp. It was either locked or stuck. No telling where the key was after all these years. If Lily had used the chest for a hiding place, she may have hidden the key somewhere in the attic, but that could take forever to find. Rummaging through the drawers in her grandmother's old sewing machine, she found a pair of scissors and used one of the blades to pry open the fastener.

The scent of cedar was fainter than she would have expected. After so many years in a musty attic, the wood probably needed to be oiled or treated. She sat down on the rough plank flooring and proceeded to empty the contents one item at a time—her grandfather's uniform, the folded flag that had been presented to her grandmother at his memorial service, a box of metals and photographs. But nothing remotely like a secret stash. Was she relieved or disappointed? Veda wondered. She hadn't expected to find anything, and maybe that was a good thing. Maybe now she could put Jon Redmond and the doubts he'd created out of her head.

She started to return everything to the chest when she noticed a small notch in the bottom. She slipped her finger in the slot and lifted. The wood came up, revealing a space underneath the base large enough to accommodate an old cigar box like the one her grandmother had used to store buttons.

Veda felt a mixture of excitement and trepidation as she removed the box from its hiding space. She shook the contents without opening the lid. Not buttons, she decided. So what was inside? And why was she hesitating to find out?

Assuming the box contained keepsakes from Lily's se-

cret affair, how had she known about the false bottom in
the chest unless their grandmother had told her? Veda had
never been jealous of Lily's beauty or popularity, but she felt
a little sting that in all the times she and her grandmother
had gone through her grandfather's things together, she'd
never once shared that secret with Veda. In the next instant,
she chided herself for being petty. She and her grandmother
had always been close. Sharing a secret with Lily had probably been her way of trying to cultivate a relationship with
her more aloof granddaughter.

And why did it matter anyway, when she might be holding Lily's secrets in her hand?

Opening the lid, she quickly sorted through the contents—a thin stack of letters tied with a pink ribbon, a
dried rose, a gold heart pendant, a small bottle of perfume
and a myriad of other items that had no meaning to Veda.
At the very bottom of the stash, she found the mystery
man's photograph. A snapshot that looked to have caught
him unaware.

She peered down at his profile as recognition teased.
She couldn't immediately place him or recall his name.
Then she had it. He'd been the high-school guidance counselor when Lily was a senior. She'd worked in his office
during her free periods and sometimes after school. Veda
had only been a sophomore then, but she'd already chosen
a career path and had no need of a guidance counselor, or
so she'd told herself.

What was his name? Michael Something-or-other. He'd
had an odd surname. Legion. No, Legend. Michael Legend.
She tried to remember everything she could about the man.
He'd been young, good-looking and exceedingly charming.
Some of her girlfriends had joked about his name behind

his back. *A legend in the sack. A legendary kisser.* The silliness had gone on and on.

Veda had only ever interacted with the man one time that she could remember. She'd stopped by his office after school looking for her sister. He and Lily had been behind his desk standing very close to one another. Veda remembered how they had both looked up startled when she came through the door. And how quickly Lily had stepped away as if she'd been caught in the act. Which, in hindsight, maybe she had been.

Far from the excitement Veda had initially experienced on discovering her sister's hiding place, she now felt unnerved and a little nauseous. She closed the lid and stared at the box for the longest time, debating on whether or not to return it to the cedar chest. She had a bad feeling that she had opened a Pandora's box. If she put it back, no one else would ever have to know. But she'd know. And as she sat there in deep contemplation, Jon's voice whispered through her head: *What if I'm right and Lily's killer is still out there? What if he resurfaced seventeen years later to murder my brother?*

An uncanny silence fell over the attic. Veda lifted her head as something clawed at her senses. She could have sworn she heard footfalls in the stairwell.

She turned slowly, peering through the dust motes floating in sunlight. Someone stood in the shadows watching her. Her heart skipped a beat. Even as the image of Lily's bad man flitted through her head, she realized the watcher was, in fact, her grandmother's old dressmaker form. She tried to laugh at how easily she'd fallen prey to her imagination, but her nerves still bristled with warning. She got up and slipped across the creaky floor to glance down the stairwell. The door at the bottom still gaped open.

Descending a few steps, she called out, "Is someone down there?"

When no one responded, she returned to the attic, placed her grandfather's things back inside the chest and slid it against the wall. Then she gathered up the cigar box and headed downstairs to decide what she wanted to do next.

Owen stood on the other side of the stairwell door. She gasped and visibly started when she saw him.

He gave her a strange look. "What's got into you?"

"After everything that's happened, do you even have to ask?" She took a moment to catch her breath. "Why didn't you answer when I called out?"

"Maybe because I didn't hear you. I just now came upstairs looking for you. I saw the attic door open and figured Mom had forgotten to close it. She's forgetting a lot of things these days, in case you hadn't noticed."

"She's had a lot on her mind. We all have."

His gaze traveled up the narrow staircase behind her. "What were you doing up there, anyway?"

"Nothing," she evaded. "I'm scanning some photographs for Mom. I thought I might find Grandma's old picture box up there."

He nodded to the cigar box. "Is that it?"

"No, just a few things I found while I was up there." She turned and struggled with the door latch for a moment.

He reached around her and fiddled with the mechanism. "Is that thing still broken?"

"There was never anything wrong with it. It's just old." She made sure the door was secure before she turned back to him. "Why were you looking for me?"

"Nate and I are leaving. Mom's still resting. Can you stick around until she wakes up?"

"Yes, of course. I had planned on it, anyway."

He lifted a hand and scratched the back of his neck. "We didn't get a chance to talk at lunch. I didn't want to say anything in front of Mom."

"What is it?"

"You were right. The police came to talk to me."

Her pulse quickened. "What happened?"

"Nothing. They just showed up at the apartment, asked a few questions and left."

"That's it?"

"Yeah. But that's not why I wanted to talk to you. Something has been bothering me about our conversation the other morning when you told me about Tony's murder. What was the real reason you came to see me?"

Veda said in surprise, "That was the real reason."

"But why the urgency? Why didn't you just call like Nate did?"

"I did call."

"And then you felt the need to rush over to Ashley's apartment to see me in person. Why?"

Veda had the unpleasant notion that she was walking into some kind of trap. She chose her words carefully. "I was there when you had that fight with Tony. I heard what you said to him. I knew it would eventually get back to the police, and I wanted you to be prepared if and when they came to question you. Or, worse, to arrest you."

"And I told you, Uncle Marcus would never let it get that far."

"He's not in charge of the investigation, and his powers as chief of police aren't unlimited. He might not have a say in the matter. Just because they left after they questioned you doesn't mean they won't be back."

"You sound as if you think I *should* be arrested."

"Don't be ridiculous."

Her brother fell silent. His gaze was still on her, but he seemed lost in deep contemplation.

She decided to press him. "What else is on your mind, Owen?"

He gave her a quizzical look. "Do you think I did it?"

The point-blank question startled her. "No, of course not. As I said, I want you to be prepared, that's all. Hopefully, they'll catch the real killer soon, and we can get back to normal."

He scoffed at that notion. "We haven't been a normal family since Tony Redmond killed our sister."

His words were truer than she wanted to admit.

He leaned a shoulder against the wall. "You still think *he* did it, don't you?"

She felt on the defensive, all of a sudden. "Why would you even ask that?"

"You never seemed as certain as the rest of us. I always wondered if you had a little crush on Tony."

Veda thought he must be joking at first, but his expression was dead serious. "That's ludicrous."

"Is it, though? Don't you remember how he was back then? Big football star walking through the halls as if he owned the whole school. Girls swooning right and left. What you said at the trial about Lily seeing someone behind his back. I was glad that came out. He needed to be taken down a peg or two."

"Somebody has certainly done that now," she murmured.

"Don't expect me to shed any tears."

Nate had said something similar when he called her with

the news. Veda understood their reaction, but their cold-ness still troubled her.

"Let's get one thing clear," she said. "I didn't have a crush on Tony Redmond. He and Lily were together from the time they were in junior high. Everyone, including me, thought they were the perfect couple."

"And look how that turned out. People are rarely what they seem, Veda."

"That's a cynical outlook."

He shrugged. "Doesn't mean it's not true."

She started to move past him, but he caught her arm. She glanced up. "What is it?"

"Why were you so jumpy when you saw me just now?"

"That's easy." She pulled away from him. "You don't re-member the time you locked me in the attic for the better part of an afternoon? I was so freaked out I tried to climb through a window onto the roof. I could have fallen and broken my neck."

His eyes glinted. "I never copped to that."

"I know. But despite what you told Mom, that door couldn't have locked itself."

"Sure, it could. See?" He opened the door and dem-onstrated how the catch could fall into place with only a slight bump.

"Nice try," she said. "It had to have been you or Nate. No one else was in the house."

"And naturally you assumed it was me." He gave her an enigmatic smile. "I'll let you in on a little secret. Nate wasn't always the good son."

VEDA WAITED UNTIL she was certain her brothers were gone before heading downstairs. The conversation with Owen had left her unsettled. He'd been in such a strange mood. Did he really think she'd had a crush on Tony Redmond, or was he just trying to goad her for some reason? And what did he mean about Nate not always being the good son?

Downstairs, the quiet of the house only deepened her unease. She wanted nothing more than to drive straight home so that she could examine Lily's secrets in private. The letters especially intrigued her, but she reined in her curiosity because she didn't want to take the chance that her mother might see them. Instead, she decided to store the cigar box in her car and put the contents out of her mind for now.

She went out the front door, letting the screen door close softly behind her. Then she stopped cold when she saw her uncle coming up the brick walkway. He was in uniform today, she noticed. Everything pressed and polished with sunlight glinting off his badge as he stepped onto the porch.

"Marcus! I didn't hear you drive up."

He cocked his head in disapproval. "So it's just *Marcus* now, is it? Since when did I stop being your uncle?"

The question caught her by surprise, and she tried to think of an inoffensive answer. "I never even noticed when I dropped it. I suppose after I went to work for the coroner's office, I started thinking of you more as a colleague than a relative. I certainly never meant any disrespect."

He flashed a brief grin. "None taken. I'm just messing with you."

Was it her imagination or was everyone acting odd today? The teasing banter didn't suit Marcus, and the awkwardness made Veda uncomfortable.

"Good one," she offered gamely. "What are you doing here anyway?"

"Guess that means I missed lunch."

"You did. Sorry. Nate and Owen just left."

"Where's Janie?"

"She's resting. Would you like something to drink while you wait?"

"I didn't come to see your mother. Although, I'm glad you and your brothers took my advice to heart. It's nice that you're spending more time with her. It's important to protect her from what's coming."

Veda frowned at his ominous tone. "What *is* coming?"

"Like I told you at the cemetery, there's going to be talk. No way around it. All those rumors about Lily's partying and drug use are bound to resurface. I'll do what I can to head off the worst of it, but you said yourself this is the information age. Everything ends up on the internet sooner or later."

She glanced down at the cigar box, keenly aware of the secrets she held in her hand. "If you didn't come to see Mom, why are you here?"

"I was hoping to have a word with you."

"Is this about Owen?" she asked anxiously.

"Now, why would you think that?"

"He said the police came to his apartment. I assume you knew."

He shrugged. "Routine interview. Nothing to worry about."

"Are you sure?"

His tone turned impatient. "I didn't come here to talk to you about Owen."

"Then, what is it?"

He paused for a moment. "You still consider yourself a Campion, don't you?"

She couldn't help but bristle. "What kind of a question is that?"

"I'm just trying to figure out where your loyalties lie."

"You came all the way out here to ask me that?"

"You've been away for a long time. I need to know you're still one of us."

Veda felt a rush of anger, blunted by the prickle of unease at her nape. Why was he really here? "It's funny you should ask that. Owen said something similar when I went to tell him that Tony Redmond had been murdered."

"I told you and Nate to keep your mouths shut about that murder until I said otherwise."

She took a breath and tempered her response. "I didn't know that included family. You sent Nate to tell Mom, so I figured Owen also had a right to know."

"That was different. I was worried about her health. You should have checked with me before talking to Owen."

Her disquiet deepened. "Why? You said there was nothing to worry about."

"There isn't. I'll take care of your brother like I always have."

Even as a kid, Veda had never felt particularly comfortable in her uncle's presence. A part of her resented the fact that he'd made himself scarce after their dad died when he could have made things easier for their mom. Not that it had been his responsibility, but still. He'd since grown close to her brothers. Nate had even followed in his footsteps, and Owen evidently thought he would keep him out of jail. Sometimes Veda felt like a stranger in her own family, but she supposed that was her fault. For whatever reason, she'd decided to go her own way after college. She was only now realizing what those solitary years had cost her.

Marcus nodded to the cigar box. "You've got a death grip on that thing. Should I be worried about what's inside?"

"I'm scanning some photos for Mom." She was relieved he didn't demand to see the contents. "But that's not the reason you're here. Maybe it's time to tell me why you're suddenly questioning my loyalty."

He glanced toward the screen door as if to make sure they were still alone. "I've been hearing some things that have me worried. I wanted to get your side before I started jumping to any conclusions."

She scowled across the porch at him. "You're hearing things about me?"

"About you and Jon Redmond."

Her heart thudded in spite of herself. That explained the loyalty question. "What are you talking about?"

"Not much goes on in this town that I don't find out about," he said. "Someone sees something curious or troubling, they report back to me. Jon Redmond's car was spotted parked outside your house last evening."

"It's not a crime to have visitors."

"It's not a crime," he agreed. "But I need to know what he's up to."

She stifled her irritation and tried to keep her voice neutral. "He's not up to anything as far as I know. He came to ask me about the autopsy."

"The autopsy?" Marcus looked skeptical. "Why come to you? You made it clear you wouldn't be involved in the postmortem. Why not go straight to Bader?"

"Apparently, he wanted a second opinion. He thinks Dr. Bader's work has been subpar lately. He said he's been taking on a lot of outside contracts. Spreading himself too thin and cutting corners. Is that true?"

"It's no secret the man's getting on in years," Marcus said. "Which is why I'm hoping you'll reconsider a permanent position. We could use someone with your education and experience at the coroner's office."

"I told you I'd think about it." She hesitated. "Is that all you wanted to know?"

"Not quite. Have you talked to Jon since last night?"

"No. Why?"

"Someone broke into his apartment, probably just after he left your house. The suspect was still inside when he got home. Worked him over pretty good with a baseball bat."

Veda's heart skipped a beat in spite of herself. "Is he okay?"

Her uncle's tone was indifferent. "He's got a few cuts and bruises, but he'll live."

She tried to digest the revelation without appearing to be alarmed. "Do you know who did it?"

"Perp fled the scene, apparently without taking anything. Jon claims he didn't recognize him. Said it was too dark in the apartment and the guy might have been wearing a mask."

"You sound as if you don't believe him."

"I don't think he's been honest about a lot of things," Marcus said. "I'm hoping you'll be able to help shed some light."

"I don't see how. I didn't even know about the break-in until just now. Do you think it's connected to Tony's murder?"

"We're looking into that possibility."

"We?" She gave him a pointed stare. "Isn't Garrett Calloway heading up the investigation? I thought you were going to distance yourself."

"He's lead on the murder case, but I'm still the police chief last time I checked. Every crime in this town falls under my purview. Besides, I wanted to hear Jon's account before he had a chance to change his story."

"Why would he change his story?"

"He's involved in this somehow," Marcus insisted. "I just haven't figured out the details."

"You think he had something to do with his brother's murder?" Veda's tone was almost scolding. "Come on. You don't really believe that. Why would he go to so much trouble to get Tony out of prison only to turn around and shoot him?"

"You tell me."

"He wouldn't," Veda said. "That's your answer."

"I never said he pulled the trigger. But he knows something." Marcus studied her features as if searching for a telltale sign of her complicity. "Before you hear it from someone else, I may as well tell you that he and I got into it while I was at his apartment."

"Physically?"

"We had words. He has a knack for pushing my buttons, but that's neither here nor there at the moment. I want to go back to your meeting with him last evening. Did he happen to mention Clay Stipes?"

Now they were veering into territory that Jon might consider confidential, but Veda wasn't going to lie about their conversation. "He said he didn't trust Stipes, but that's hardly a surprise."

"What was the context?"

"He believes the person Lily was involved with had motive to kill her. That's also not a surprise."

Marcus scoffed. "The so-called mystery man."

"He was real. Lily told me about him." She glanced down at the cigar box, then looked away. "Did the police ever look for him?"

"Of course we did, but there wasn't anything to go on. No name, no description." He shrugged. "We couldn't produce him out of thin air."

"They didn't find anything when they searched through Lily's belongings?"

His gaze sharpened. "Don't you think you would have known if we had?"

"I've just been wondering. It seems like she would have kept a diary or journal. Something."

"You said on the stand she wanted to keep his identity a secret. But we're getting sidetracked," he said with a scowl. "What business did Jon have with Clay Stipes?"

"Stipes claims to know the mystery man's name. He offered to disclose his identity for money."

Her uncle stared at her dumbfounded. "How the hell would Clay Stipes know anything about a man Lily was allegedly involved with seventeen years ago?"

"Apparently, Tony approached him in prison because Stipes had a reputation for being able to dig up information. That's really all I know. Why are you so interested in Stipes, anyway? Do you think he's the one who broke into Jon's apartment?"

"It's possible."

"Do you think he had something to do with Tony's murder?"

"Everyone is a suspect as far as I'm concerned. But I've always had a problem with the timing of that murder. Clay Stipes hits town, and a few days later Tony Redmond turns up dead. My gut tells me they were cooking up something together. Maybe one double-crossed the other. I don't know. But I have a feeling Jon Redmond knows more than he's telling. He may even be in on it, too."

Veda was quick to defend Jon. "You think he'd be involved in something criminal? I don't believe it."

"See how persuasive he can be?" Her uncle made no effort to conceal his scorn. "He's a prosecutor. It's his job to make people believe him."

Veda switched tactics before her uncle jumped to even more conclusions about her and Jon Redmond. "What did the two of you argue about at his apartment?"

"He implied that I conspired with the former DA to conceal evidence in Tony's case."

"Did you?"

His mouth tightened. "You really want to go down that road with me, Veda Louise?"

His use of her middle name annoyed her. Only her brothers were allowed to call her that. "I'm not trying to pick a fight," she said. "But the department must have known about Tony's tox screen and the witness account of someone fleeing his truck. Both pieces of evidence went missing before the trial, and they provided the basis for his appeal."

Marcus didn't bat an eye when he answered. "As far as I know, everything was turned over to the DA's office."

"But no one said anything when he failed to disclose key pieces to the defense."

"That's not our job," Marcus countered. "We interview witnesses and gather the evidence. What the prosecutor does once he brings charges is his business. Besides, why would we say anything? We wanted that bastard behind bars as much as anyone."

Veda asked in a quiet voice, "And if he didn't do it?"

"He did it. Never a doubt in my mind." His eyes glittered dangerously. "I take it you don't feel the same."

"Whether he was guilty or not, he deserved a fair trial."

"You can say that after what he did to your own sister?"

"This isn't about family loyalty," she said. "It's about doing the right thing."

"The right thing." He shook his head in disgust. "You sound just like Jon Redmond. He's making you doubt what you know in your heart to be true. Let me give you a piece of advice. Every time he tries to crawl inside your head, you remind yourself of what his brother did to your sister. He used a utility knife. The same one he bought to cut carpet. Not quick, not painless—"

Her mother's gasp stopped him midsentence. Veda whirled to find her standing on the other side of the screen gazing out at them. "Mom! How long have you been there?"

She opened the door and stepped out on the porch without answering.

Marcus straightened from the railing. "Janie, I'm sorry. I didn't know you were there—"

"Just stop, Marcus." Her mother's harsh tone surprised Veda.

"I was just trying to explain to Veda why she shouldn't trust Jon Redmond."

"You let me talk to my daughter." Her mother turned. "Why would you ever trust the man who twisted the law to get Lily's killer out of prison?"

"It's not about trust," Veda said. "And he didn't have to twist anything because the former DA gave him plenty of ammunition. Jon's always proclaimed his brother's innocence. That isn't new."

"He got that piece of—" Marcus self-edited in her mother's presence. "He got his brother out of prison. That should have been enough for him, but he just can't let it go."

Her mother's attention was still on Veda. "You don't believe Tony was innocent, do you?"

Veda grew apprehensive. There was a glitter of something she didn't want to define in her mother's eyes. "He's dead. What does it matter what I believe?"

"It matters to me." She moved across the porch and took Veda's arms, her voice dropping to a near whisper. "Don't you understand? I need for that man to be guilty."

Chapter Nine

Veda was still distraught by the time she finally drove home. She couldn't get her mother's anguish out of her mind. The look in her eyes…the desperate plea. *Don't you understand? I need for that man to be guilty.*

The thoughts churning through Veda's head made her physically ill. For a moment, she thought she might have to pull over. The last few weeks had been stressful, and the knots in her stomach had only multiplied after Tony's murder. She told herself to take a deep breath and get a grip. No one in her family had done anything wrong. Their attitude toward Tony Redmond was understandable. Hadn't she felt a momentary relief upon hearing about his death? It was only natural that her mother needed someone to blame, and the evidence against Tony had been overwhelming.

But the other side of the coin had started to nag. He'd spent his whole adult life in prison only to be murdered when he got out. The very notion of his innocence made the reality of those seventeen years almost unbearable.

Yes, Veda thought. We need for that man to be guilty.

Jon was sitting on her porch steps when she got home. She wanted to send him away, but she was the one who had impulsively called him after leaving her mother's house. "I have some news," she'd told him. She should have known he wouldn't be able to wait.

He rose when she came up the walkway, his expression shifting from expectant to worry. "Are you okay? You look—"

She tried to take his concern lightly. "Like death warmed-over?"

"Upset." He stood in front of her but made no move to touch her. At that moment, she wasn't sure how she would have reacted if he had. Something was happening between them. She couldn't deny the flare of attraction in his presence, but that spark was doomed by the insurmountable history that stood between them.

"What's wrong?"

"Nothing." She shook off a sudden melancholy. "This whole business…it's brought back a lot of memories."

His tone noticeably cooled. "By *this whole business*, do you mean my brother's murder?"

She was immediately ashamed. "I'm sorry. I didn't mean to sound so callous."

"I get it. To you, he's still your sister's killer."

She looked him in the eyes. "I can't help how I feel."

He glanced away, searching the street for a moment. "I understand."

But do you? Do you have any idea how hard this is for me? Her loyalty to her family was being questioned even as Jon's unwavering belief in his brother's innocence picked at her doubts. She was being pulled in two different directions, and the tension was taking a toll.

She took in the bruises on his face and the bandage above his eyebrow. Sympathy tugged despite her trepidation, and she softened her tone. "I heard what happened at your apartment. Are *you* okay?"

His gaze came back to her. "Marcus told you?"

She nodded. "He stopped by my mom's house a little while ago. He said the assailant was in your apartment when you got home. He attacked you with a baseball bat."

He smiled, but there was no humor in his eyes. "That's not exactly how it happened, but I'm fine. No permanent damage except to my ego."

"It's nothing to joke about," she said. "You could have been seriously injured or killed." She winced as soon as the words were out of her mouth. Both families had suffered too many tragedies. The thought of Jon meeting an untimely demise triggered an emotion Veda didn't want to explore. "Do you know who did it? Or what they were after? Marcus said the suspect fled without taking anything."

"I didn't get a good look at him, but I have a feeling it has to do with Tony's murder. And with everything you and I talked about last evening. Someone doesn't want us digging up the past."

"But you've been doing that for years," she pointed out.

"Not like this. The appeal was focused on prosecutorial misconduct. Now we're trying to find out the truth about Lily's murder, and it feels as if we may be getting close."

We may be getting close? She suppressed the urge to remind him yet again that just because she'd heard him out didn't mean she accepted his claim. Doubt about Tony's guilt was one thing. Embracing a full exoneration quite another. But maybe that was Marcus talking. Like it or not, her uncle had hit a sore spot when he questioned her loyalty.

She glanced down at the cigar box in her hand. "Let's go inside."

They climbed the porch steps together. Veda couldn't help glancing over her shoulder as she unlocked the front door. She wondered who had reported Jon's car to her uncle. The notion of a neighbor keeping tabs didn't sit well.

He followed her through the small house to the breakfast nook that looked out on the shady backyard. She surreptitiously studied him as she moved aside folders and her laptop on the table. Once she got past the cuts and bruises, she noticed the circles under his eyes were less pronounced, and he didn't look as stricken with shock as he had the day before. His casual attire of collared shirt and trousers made her overly aware of her everyday summer uniform of sandals, jeans and a T-shirt.

She moved around him into the kitchen. "Can I get you something to drink?"

"I'm fine, thanks." He sat down at the table and folded his hands. "I was surprised to get your call."

"Why?" She took a seat across from him and placed the cigar box on the tabletop. "I told you I'd take another look through Lily's things to put your mind at ease."

"And?"

"I found this." She tapped the lid. "Turns out you were right. She did have a secret hiding place."

His expression turned anxious. "What's inside?"

"A photograph of the mystery man, a handful of letters, a few other odds and ends. But no diary."

He glanced up. "Wait a minute. You found a photograph of the secret boyfriend?"

"I think so." Then she added with a note of caution, "You shouldn't get too excited. I haven't read the letters yet, but I doubt any of this will turn out to be a smoking gun."

"I wasn't expecting a smoking gun. Like I said last night, one good lead is all we need."

She opened the box and removed the photograph. "You can only see his profile in this shot. He seems completely unaware of the camera. I have a feeling Lily took it without him knowing. If what we suspect about their relationship is true, he probably discouraged any damning evidence of their affair."

"What about the letters?"

"One thing at a time." She slid the photograph across the table. "Do you recognize him?"

He picked up the image and gave it a careful examination. "I don't think so. Should I?"

"Not necessarily. You would have graduated high school a couple of years before he was hired."

"He was a teacher?"

"Guidance counselor. His name is Michael Legend."

Jon lifted a brow before he dropped his gaze to the photo. "That would be a hard last name to live up to."

"Probably not for him," Veda said. "If memory serves, he thought pretty highly of himself."

"I take it you knew him."

"I knew who he was, of course, but I never had any interaction with him. I didn't think I needed the services of a guidance counselor," she added with a deprecating smile. "I thought I knew everything back then."

"Didn't we all?"

Her heart gave a funny lurch when he smiled back. She glanced down at the box. "A lot of my friends had crushes on him, but I never heard anything untoward about his behavior with students."

Jon placed the photo on the table. "So, this is the mystery man."

"I would assume so. Why else would she have kept his image hidden in the attic underneath a false bottom in our grandmother's old cedar chest?"

He looked both surprised and impressed. "That sounds a little like finding a needle in a haystack. What made you think to look there?"

"Not *what*. *Who*. Lily told me."

He said carefully, "Not literally, I'm guessing."

Her smile was brief. "No, her ghost didn't come to me. It was something I remembered when I was in her room yesterday. She had this recurring nightmare as a kid about someone coming through her window and sitting on her bed to watch her sleep. She called him the bad man, and she said thunder summoned him. She used to hide at the back of her closet and cover her ears to block the sound."

"No wonder she was afraid of storms."

Veda nodded. "Although, I don't know if her fear of storms or the nightmare came first. Anyway, there was a big storm on the night of her eighteenth birthday. She'd been out with Tony and came home late. When I got up to go to the bathroom, I heard a whimper coming from her closet. The way she sounded... I'd never heard anything like it. I was scared to go closer even though I knew my sister was inside."

"Why did it frighten you?" Jon asked, his tone still guarded as if unsure how he was supposed to react to her revelations.

She shivered. "It sounded like a hushed howl, if you can imagine such a thing. Like a trapped or wounded animal."

"That must have been—"

"Hair-raising?" Veda held out her arm. "I still get goose bumps when I think about it."

"What did you do?"

"I was sixteen years old, practically an adult, and yet I had to make myself crawl into that closet. Sounds silly now. Cowardly, even."

He met her gaze across the table. "No, it doesn't."

She took a breath. "You say that, but you don't know how badly I wanted to run back to my room and pretend I never heard that cry."

"But you didn't."

"I couldn't. I had to make sure she was okay."

"Was she?"

"She wasn't physically hurt, but she was distressed. She told me she had the dream again. That the bad man came through the window and sat on her bed while she pretended to sleep. She said he had a *smell*."

"What kind of smell?"

"Like our grandmother's old cedar chest."

"Ah." A light dawned in his eyes.

"You see where I'm going with this. She'd never mentioned a scent before, and she seemed surprised because she said the devil should smell like sulfur."

That took him aback. "The devil?"

"I know." Veda rubbed her hand along the chill bumps. "After she told me about the dream, she confessed to seeing someone behind Tony's back. She said they were planning to go away together." She swallowed past the sudden knot in her throat. How different things might have turned out if she'd been able to convince Lily not to see him again. "Even when we were little, she implied the bad man came because of something she'd done. It seems so obvious now, but it never occurred to me back then. The bad man came to punish her when *she* was bad. He was a manifestation of her guilty conscience."

"That makes sense," Jon said. "It's disturbing, but it makes sense."

"Especially for Lily. Things weighed on her even as a kid. The bad man came back on her birthday because she knew the affair was wrong. I think her subconscious gave him the scent of our grandmother's cedar chest because she hid the evidence of her wrongdoing inside. Maybe she'd been thinking about the chest before she went to sleep that night. She may even have been up in the attic before the storm hit."

"What a heavy burden she must have carried."

Veda felt the sting of unexpected tears at his empathy. That he could be nonjudgmental in the face of everything that had happened was extraordinary. "I never wanted to believe all those terrible rumors that surfaced about my sister during the trial. I thought people were just being gossipy and mean-spirited, and I blamed myself for breaking her confidence on the witness stand. But an affair with a married man…that's serious. That behavior can't be chalked up to youthful indiscretion."

"First of all, you were under oath," he reminded her. "You had to tell the truth. As for the rumors, whether or not they were true, you shouldn't let anyone diminish the memories you have of your sister or how much you loved her. And don't think too harshly of her for being human. She was young and in love. People do foolish things at that age. At any age. God knows I have my share of regrets."

"You didn't have an affair, did you?" She was only half-joking.

He took the question seriously. "No. But I rushed into marriage when I was in law school. It was an especially stressful time, and I thought our being together would help me get through it. It was selfish and impulsive on my part. Not surprisingly, we only lasted a few months. Technically the split was mutual, but there's no such thing as a clean break. People make mistakes, and people get hurt. You learn to live with regret and move on."

"Lily never had a chance to move on."

"Neither did Tony."

Veda fell silent, both stunned and touched by his confession. Never in a million years could she have imagined a scenario that brought Jon Redmond to her kitchen table, let alone sharing an intimate interlude from his past. She wanted to take it at face value. Just his way of making her see Lily's behavior in a kinder light. Yet a part of her still wondered if he had an ulterior motive. *When he tries to crawl inside your head, you remind yourself of what his brother did to your sister.*

"You mentioned letters," he said.

She removed the stack from the box and handed them to him.

He hesitated before accepting them. "Don't you want to read them first?"

"I don't have it in me right now. I broke my sister's confidence once. Breaching her privacy seems a bridge too far at the moment."

"But you're allowing me to read them. What's the difference?"

She sighed. "Someone has to do it, and I'd rather it be you than me. Just scan the contents, and tell me if there's anything I need to know."

He looked doubtful as he untied the ribbon and sorted through the envelopes. "No address or postmark. Just her name."

"Yes, I noticed. They probably had a special place for leaving letters and notes to one another. His office, her locker..." Veda shrugged. "They needed to take precautions. If anyone caught on, he would have been fired. Lily may have been past the age of consent in Mississippi, but a married teacher involved with a student would have had serious consequences. Not to mention what his wife would have done if she'd found out."

Jon removed a single page from the first envelope, scanned the text and then glanced up. "It's a love letter." He turned over the paper and examined the back. "No name, no mention of his marital status or profession. Nothing to give away his identity if the letter fell into the wrong hands. He might even have tried to disguise his handwriting. He uses a lot of printed letters rather than cursive. It doesn't flow naturally."

"I imagine he was careful about a lot of things. They both were. I never had a clue until Lily told me." Veda made a rotating motion with her finger, indicating he should move on to the next envelope.

He quickly read through the rest of the letters, lingering on the last one until her curiosity got the better of her.

"What is it?"

"It's more or less a Dear John letter." He folded the paper and handed it back to her. "You should read this one."

She took the page and reluctantly skimmed through the brief lines, then went back to the top and reread everything more carefully. Her voice trembled with emotion when she spoke. "He didn't just break up with her. He threatened her."

"Some might interpret it as more of a warning," Jon said with a note of caution.

She read some of the more egregious lines aloud. *"Stop calling me. Stop writing to me. Stop watching my house. If you ever come near my property again, you'll find out just how angry I can get."* Veda glanced up. "You don't call that a threat? Whose side are you on, anyway?"

"I didn't know we were choosing sides."

"There have always been sides," she said.

"You're right. But the only side we should be concerned about this time is the truth."

Her annoyance faded as she wondered how to broach another subject. "You mean that, don't you?"

"Of course, I do."

"With that in mind… I need to ask you something."

He tied the ribbon around the letters and handed them back to her. "What is it?"

"Did you know the police talked to Owen?"

"I wasn't informed, but I can't say I'm surprised. A lot of people knew about that fight, Veda. A lot of people heard him threaten my brother."

She bit her lip. "Yet you haven't once accused him of Tony's murder."

"I've maintained all along that the same person who killed Lily killed Tony. That wasn't Owen."

She let out a breath. "You don't know how much it means to hear you say that."

"I think I do."

Their gazes held for the longest time until she finally glanced away. "What do we do now?"

"First off, we don't get ahead of ourselves."

"Meaning?"

"If those letters are from Legend, they paint him in a bad light, no question. But as you pointed out earlier, they're not a smoking gun. Nothing in them leads directly to him. That's okay. Neither murder was ever going to be solved overnight, but at least now we have a significant lead. Thanks to you, we have a place to start."

Since when had their roles reversed? Veda wondered. She was supposed to be the cautious, skeptical voice of reason.

"I can't help thinking about the implication," she said. "Lily kept calling and writing. Watching his house. She must have been desperate for his attention."

"She had a broken heart," Jon said.

Veda returned the letter to the stack and placed the envelopes back in the box. "Do you think his wife knew about the affair?"

"I don't know, but he was probably afraid Lily would tell her. The letters may not be evidence of murder, but they are proof of an affair and if we can tie them back to him, that gives him motive."

"But that's not enough to take to the police, is it?"

"We could have a signed confession and it wouldn't be enough for your uncle," Jon said with a bitter edge. "I can't do anything officially, but we're not without resources. The first thing we do is find out everything we can about this guy." He took out his phone.

"You're not calling Clay Stipes, are you?"

He looked up with a scowl. "Why would you think that?"

"You said he was good at digging up information."

"No, *he* said that. Clay Stipes is about the last person I'd ever trust him with sensitive information. We do this on our own, and we start with something safe like an internet search."

Veda slid her laptop toward him. "Use this, then. It'll be easier for both of us to read the results."

While he started the search, she got up and went into the kitchen to pour two glasses of iced tea. When she brought them back to the table, he said, "No bourbon this time?"

"We both need to keep a clear head. Tea is all you get."

"Fair enough." He left the drink untouched as he studied the screen.

Veda came around to look over his shoulder. "What did you find?"

"Quite a lot, actually. He's the vice president of a company that owns hotels and casinos along the Gulf Coast. The owner and CEO is a man named Armand Fontenot. According to this write-up in *Mississippi Business Report*, Legend has been married to Kathryn Fontenot for the past eighteen years. Apparently, Clay Stipes was right about one thing. Our mystery man married into a wealthy, influential family. He had a lot to lose if his wife ever got wind of an affair."

Veda straightened. "You said he and his wife have been married for the past eighteen years?"

"Assuming the information in this article is accurate and up-to-date."

"That means he was practically a newlywed when he started the affair with Lily." She moved back around the table and sat down. "What kind of man does that?"

"A weak man with more ambition than morals." Jon closed the laptop lid. "I'll go back to the office and see what else I can dig up. I doubt he has a criminal record, but you never know."

"And then what?"

"Then, I pay him a visit. If I can catch him off guard,

so much the better. It'll be interesting to see how he reacts when he finds out I'm Tony Redmond's brother."

Now it was Veda who offered a note of caution. "What happened to not getting ahead of ourselves?"

He shrugged off her concern. "I'm not going to accuse him of murder. Just rattle his cage a little."

"And what if he is the murderer? What's to keep him from coming after you?"

"Let's hope he does." The glitter in his eyes unnerved her.

"Maybe he already has," she suggested.

"You mean the break-in? The thought crossed my mind. But if that person wanted me dead, he would have come armed with more than a flashlight."

Veda ran her hand across the top of the cigar box. "Then, let me come with you. You want to see how he reacts when he finds out you're Tony Redmond's brother? Well, I want to see his face when I tell him I'm Lily Campion's sister."

He hesitated. "That may not be the best idea."

She was instantly on the defensive. "Why is it a good idea for you and not for me?"

"It may not be a good idea for either of us," he said. "Let's not forget two people have been murdered."

"Which means neither of us should do anything impulsive. Or alone."

"Okay," he conceded. "What do you have in mind?"

She settled back in her chair. "We take the night and think it through. Then we come up with a game plan. We figure out when and where to approach him and what we want to say to him."

The blue eyes gleamed with a different emotion. "So it's *we* now?"

"You're the one who started tossing around that pronoun when you first came to see me. And I'll remind you that you had no problem asking me to dig through Lily's belongings."

"That didn't put you in danger."

"Maybe not, but it wasn't easy." She eyed the box of secrets. "My family would be very upset if they knew I'd found something belonging to Lily and didn't tell them. Let alone that I let you read those letters. Besides, by the sound of that article, Michael Legend is an upstanding citizen. Or at least he pretends to be. He isn't going to try anything in broad daylight in front of two witnesses."

"No, probably not. But your previous point is well-taken. We should take the night and think things through."

She gave him a dubious look. "You sound a little too agreeable. Now that you got what you wanted, you're not going to ghost me, are you?"

His expression sobered. "I would never do that. And I won't try and stop you from coming with me if you still feel the same way in the morning. I owe you that."

Would she still feel the same after a whole night to ponder the consequences? Alone with Jon Redmond in the close confines of a car might be asking for trouble. "Do we even know how to find him?"

"I'll find him." Not a trace of doubt, Veda noticed. He motioned to the cigar box as he stood. "Take care of that. Put it somewhere safe. I'd offer to take it with me, but something tells me you would never go for that."

"No, I wouldn't. This box stays with me."

"Then, take precautions. Whoever broke into my apartment might have been looking for exactly that kind of information."

She rose. "I'll find another hiding place for my sister's

secrets. And I'll make sure to lock my doors before I turn in." She didn't feel quite as confident as she sounded. This was getting serious. Tony Redmond had been murdered in cold blood, and less than twenty-four hours later Jon had been attacked in his own apartment. Someone was apparently getting desperate.

"You have my number if you need me. Day or night," he added.

She walked him to the door. He leaned a shoulder against the frame as he stared down at her. His eyes were very blue in the late-afternoon sun shining through the front windows. He looked tired, beat-up and more handsome than any man had a right to be after what he'd been through.

"Thank you," he said. "You didn't have to help me. After everything your family has been through, it couldn't have been easy."

"We've all been through a lot. And you don't need to thank me because it was the right thing to do."

"Still, what you're doing takes courage."

The way he looked at her…the way he lingered at the door…

Veda suddenly felt as if she'd swum a little too far out of her depth. "Jon…"

He smiled. "That's the first time you've used my name."

She swallowed. "Do you ever wish things could be different? Easier? Sometimes I wonder what it would be like to feel normal again."

"I wish for a lot of things." Exhaustion deepened the lines around his eyes. "And what's *normal*, anyway? We all have crosses to bear. The only thing we can do is get on with it the best we can."

"Seventeen years is a long time to get on with it."

He put a hand to her cheek. The touch shocked her. She reached up but not to swat him away. Instead, she closed her fingers over his.

Their gazes connected for the longest time. The brother of the man convicted of killing her sister. It was a loaded moment. Not just because of what had happened to their families in the past, but because of the strange camaraderie that had been born from the tragedy.

When he leaned in this time, Veda turned her head to meet his lips. It was a kiss meant to comfort and reassure, maybe even to solidify their budding relationship, but the passion that simmered beneath the surface made her tremble.

EXCUSES SWIRLED THROUGH Jon's head as he left Veda's house and strode down her walkway. The kiss didn't mean anything. Just two people offering one another a moment of comfort and understanding. A port in the storm. But the truth of the matter was he'd been attracted to Veda Campion long before he'd asked for her help. She'd been on his radar ever since he'd observed her in action in that courtroom in New Orleans. She'd been poised, professional, impressive. And gorgeous.

He hadn't expected to be so taken aback by her appearance when he first read her name on the witness list. She'd lived in the shadow of her sister's stunning good looks for as long as Jon had known her. Apparently, she was one of those people who came into her own in her thirties. She'd had on a simple black suit for court. Her blond hair had been pulled back in a bun, and she'd worn very little makeup. No jewelry. Flat shoes. Nothing in the least sexy or alluring about her attire, and yet Jon found himself leaning forward on the bench, not just to take note of her testimony but to drink in every detail of her appearance. Veda Campion, of all people, had thoroughly captured his attention.

He'd thought about looking her up after court that day, but it hadn't seemed like a good idea. Instead, he put her out of his head and went home to Atlanta, back to his fifteen-hour days and half-furnished apartment. Back to working on his brother's appeal in addition to the obligations he had with his firm. When he'd approached her at the cemetery after Tony's murder, a relationship had been the last thing on his mind. Yet even then, he couldn't deny his awareness. As much as he might try to convince himself that the kiss had been a culmination of stress, grief and anger, deep down he knew it was more than that. At least for him.

His ringtone sounded. He was still distracted and a little annoyed when he answered.

The voice on the other end said, "Jon Redmond?"

"Speaking. Who is this?"

"Come on, Jon. Don't you recognize my voice?"

The goading tone sent his irritation soaring several notches. "What do you want, Stipes?"

"Look down the street. Black car parked at the curb."

He came to a halt on the sidewalk and turned. A few houses down, Clay Stipes stood leaning against a dark sedan. When he had Jon's attention, he lifted a hand in a brief salute.

"You should thank me," he said in Jon's ear. "I parked down the street because I didn't think you'd want your girl-friend to see us together."

Jon glanced back at the house. "She's not my girlfriend. And I don't want anyone to see us together."

"Maybe not, but you'll want to hear what I have to say."

"Then, say it."

There was a brief silence. "Not over the phone. I'll hang up and wait for you."

The call ended, and Stipes gave another wave as though he were acknowledging an old friend. Jon glanced again at the house as he slipped the phone in his pocket. No sign of Veda at any of the windows. Maybe it was hubris to think she might be staring after him.

He turned back to Stipes. His instincts told him to get in the car and drive away, but instead he started down the street. Apparently, Stipes wasn't going anywhere anytime soon so he may as well have it out with him now.

Stipes straightened as he approached and nodded. "Good to see you again, Jon. I would say you're looking well, but…" He cocked his head. "How does the other guy look?"

Jon had a sudden vision of the intruder standing over him with his own baseball bat. Darkness and possibly a mask had concealed the man's identity, but going by size, history and the viciousness of the attack, he wouldn't rule out Stipes as his assailant.

He studied the man's face. No discernible cuts and bruises. Stipes looked his usual smug self, which only further irritated Jon. "How did you know where to find me?"

"Haven't you heard? It's all over town that you've been spending time with the dead girl's sister. Oh, damn. You didn't know, did you?"

Stipes was obviously trying to get a rise out of him. People could gossip all they wanted as far as Jon was concerned, but talk of that nature could make things difficult for Veda. She'd already gone out on a limb for him.

Leaning back against the car, Stipes folded his arms. "It wasn't hard to find out where she lives. Like I said, I'm good at digging up information. I figured if I waited long enough you'd turn up."

"Congratulations," Jon said. "Did you go to all that trouble for any other reason than to antagonize me? If not, then get in your car and drive back to where you came from."

"I told you before, I'm sticking around. I've still got unfinished business in this town."

"What business?"

"You need a name, and I can get it for you."

Jon allowed himself a tight smile. "It seems you think a little too highly of your skill set. Turns out, you're not the only one who knows how to dig up information. And some of us don't have to crawl through sewers to get it."

Stipes stared back, unimpressed. "So you found him, did you?"

"Found who?"

He grinned. "I guess it helps to have someone do your dirty work for you. What's her name again? Vera? Veda? She's a real looker from the glimpse I had of her on the porch. Not in her sister's league, but I wouldn't kick her out of bed."

A rush of anger burned Jon's face and curled his fingers into fists. He took a step toward Stipes before a cooler head prevailed. The man was obviously needling him on purpose, trying to provoke a physical reaction.

"I gotta hand it to you, Jon. You're more resourceful than I thought. Just one question, though. Did it ever occur to you that she might have known all along who this guy is?"

In fact, that very notion had led to the confrontation outside the courtroom seventeen years ago. Antagonizing a grieving sixteen-year-old had been a low point for Jon. Taking out his anger and frustration—not to mention his fear—on the victim's younger sister wasn't a proud moment by any measure. "Leave her out of this."

"You're quick to jump to her defense, but maybe you should consider this. She testified that Lily never mentioned the boyfriend by name. Technically, she didn't lie if she found out his name from someone else."

Jon reminded himself yet again that Clay Stipes had an agenda. But recognizing the tactic didn't make him immune. The inferences were starting to burrow under his skin as Stipes had no doubt intended. He asked the same question that Veda had asked of him. "Why would she keep his name a secret?"

"Maybe to protect her sister's reputation. Or to make sure Tony got convicted. Her whole family believed he was guilty, didn't they? Would you still feel the same way about her if you found out she could have kept your brother out of prison?"

"Her testimony didn't send Tony to prison."

"But it sure as hell provided motive." Stipes planted his hand on the trunk of his car. With very little effort, Jon could imagine his brother inside. Hands zip-tied behind his back. A gag in his mouth to stifle his pleas for mercy.

He shook off the image. "Why are you really here?"

Stipes smiled. "I came to give you a warning."

"Sure, you did."

"I'm serious. You may have dug up Michael Legend's name, but I doubt you know who he really is."

"Meaning?"

Stipes glanced down the street. "Your brother knew about this guy. We found out his identity years ago, but Tony wanted to keep it quiet. That was his call. He never said a word to anyone, including you, because he wanted to confront Legend mano a mano, if you get my drift."

"And then what?"

The dark eyes gleamed. "What do you think? I told you before, we had a deal. And before you accuse me of taking advantage of a frightened, desperate kid, I didn't have to twist his arm."

"There are many ways of twisting arms in prison," Jon said.

"Yeah, you got that right." Stipes eyed him for a long moment. "Did you know Tony went to see Legend?"

"When?"

"First week he was out. He didn't waste any time. He said he'd know if the guy was guilty just by looking him straight in the eye."

Was that true? Jon wondered. He wanted to believe Tony would have told him about the visit, but his brother had kept a lot of things from him. Maybe he was trying to protect him. Or maybe he didn't want Jon seeing what prison had turned him into.

"Why are you telling me all this now?" he asked.

Stipes shrugged. "Your brother had my back in prison. I figure I owe him one." He squinted into the sun as he waited for Jon's reaction. When none was forthcoming, he said, "I told you the guy married into money, right? His father-in-law is Armand Fontenot. He owns hotels and casinos all up and down the Gulf Coast. His headquarters are in Biloxi."

"I already know all that," Jon said. "It took me about thirty seconds to find the same information on the internet."

Stipes grinned. "What you may not know is how Fontenot got his start. Ever hear of the Dixie Mafia?"

"Anyone who grew up around here has heard of them,"

Jon said. "But their heyday was over fifty years ago. Their numbers and influence have been dwindling since the eighties."

"They may be low-key, but they're still around, still based in Biloxi last I heard. I did time with a couple of their foot soldiers. Back in the day, they specialized in contract killing. Think about how Tony ended up after he went to see Michael Legend."

Jon didn't have to think about it. His brother's murder was never far from his mind.

"What's your point?"

"If you go nosing around in that man's business, you may end up facedown in the boneyard like your brother."

Chapter Ten

The next morning, Veda was pouring her first coffee when the doorbell rang. She set the cup aside and ran fingers through her tangled hair as she headed through the house, taking a peek out the front window before she answered. Jon's car was parked at the curb directly in front of her house. She glanced up and down the street. If there was a spy in the neighborhood, her uncle would undoubtedly hear about his visit soon enough.

She had no idea why he would show up at her place before eight o'clock in the morning without calling first. Something must have happened or else he'd obtained new information. She braced herself as she drew open the door. "I wasn't expecting you so early. What's wrong?" She searched his face for signs of another attack. "Are you okay?"

"I'm fine." He seemed oblivious to the cotton robe she wore over her summer pajamas. He brushed past her before she had a chance to invite him inside. "We need to talk."

"Come right in," she muttered, but his sense of urgency deepened her anxiety. She automatically skimmed the street before closing the door behind him.

"Before we get into the specifics, I need you to know something."

His blue eyes seemed more penetrating than ever this morning. Apprehension tickled at the back of her neck. "What is it?"

"You accused me yesterday of trying to ghost you. You implied that I might try to cut you out of the investigation now that I have what I want. That's not what I'm doing. I'm just trying to keep you safe."

"Now you're starting to scare me." She tucked her loose hair behind her ears. "Does this have anything to do with the fact that Clay Stipes was waiting down the street when you left here yesterday afternoon?"

He turned in surprise. "How did you know about that?"

"I have eyes. Your car stayed parked in front of my house for a good fifteen minutes after you left. I went outside to make sure everything was okay, and I saw you talking to someone a few houses down. I didn't recognize the man, but from your body language and the intensity of the discussion, I assumed he was Stipes."

"It was," Jon confirmed.

"Your back was to me, so I knew you didn't see me," she explained. "I didn't want to stand on the sidewalk gawking and I certainly wasn't going to interrupt your conversation. I figured you'd met him down the street for a reason." She motioned for him to follow her back to the kitchen. "I decided if he had anything new to offer, you'd tell me about it. And here you are."

"Here I am." He was dressed for work in a gray suit with a dark blue silk tie that deepened the azure of his eyes. The bruises on his face were starting to fade, but he still wore a butterfly bandage over his left eye.

She said worriedly, "Have you gone back to work already?" Surely it was too soon for that, but was there any real difference in being in the office and conducting an off-the-books investigation? Both were distractions, and maybe that was what he needed at the moment. Everyone grieved in their own way.

"I'm not back full-time, but a few cases needed my attention," he said.

"I assume Tony's murder is one of them."

"Officially, I'm recused from that case. Unofficially, I made some inquiries into Michael Legend's background. That's what I want to talk to you about. Stipes did have new information. I'm not sure how much of it is relevant or even factual, but it concerned me enough to make a few phone calls."

By this time, Veda was in the kitchen getting a second cup from the cabinet. She came back over to the counter. "This sounds serious."

"It could be serious, it could be nothing." He nodded to the empty cup in her hand. "Is that for me?"

"What? Oh, right. How do you take your coffee?"

"Black is fine."

She poured the coffee and handed him a steaming cup. Then she collected her own and came around the counter. "Let's go sit outside before the heat sets in. The backyard is nice this time of morning."

Normally, she would have chosen the front porch, but she kept remembering her uncle's boast that nothing in this town got by him. She also considered excusing herself to throw on some clothes and comb her hair, but his cryptic remarks about Clay Stipes seemed more important than her appearance.

She led him through the back door and across the patio to a pair of oversize chairs strategically placed beneath a

canopy of redbud trees. Setting her cup on the table between them, she tucked up her legs and swiveled her body
to face him. "What did Stipes say, exactly?"

He took a moment to shed his jacket and tie and roll up
his sleeves. A breeze ruffled his thick hair, making Veda
wonder what it would be like to run her fingers through
those dark strands. When he sat down beside her, she could
have sworn she caught a tantalizing whiff of his soap. She
closed her eyes on a shiver.

Jon took a tentative sip of coffee, then set his cup aside
to cool. "In a nutshell, he implied that Michael Legend
has Mafia connections through his father-in-law, Armand
Fontenot."

"Mafia connections?" For a moment, she thought he
must be joking. The claim struck her as far-fetched to the
point of being comical, but she stifled a laugh when she
noted his somber expression. "You're serious? You do realize that sounds like something from a bad movie."

"It sounded implausible to me, too, when Stipes first
made the claim. Especially dropping it out of the blue the
way he did."

"Especially coming from Clay Stipes," she said with a
grimace. "Weren't you the one who told me you couldn't
believe a word out of his mouth?"

"Yes, but I thought it worth looking into if for no other
reason than to disprove his lie. I made a few local inquiries,
and then first thing this morning I called a friend of mine
who works in the Harrison County DA's Office. He said it
was fairly common knowledge around Biloxi that Fontenot
got his start with mob money. That got me to thinking about
something else Stipes said. He reminded me of the way my
brother was murdered. He implied it was a professional hit."

Any bemusement Veda had fled. "Actually, that was Detective Calloway's conclusion, as well. According to him, most of the homicides he's dealt with since moving down here involved drugs or domestic disputes. Tony's murder was different. He said it looked like a professional hit, and you called it an execution."

"Because it was." Jon's voice remained calm, but cold anger flickered in his eyes, reminding Veda that when it came to the murder of a loved one, few were immune to the baser instincts of rage and revenge. Not Jon. Not her brothers. Not even her mother, apparently.

She pulled her robe around her as if she could block her unsettling thoughts. "Let me play devil's advocate for a minute. You've said all along that you think the same person killed both Tony and Lily. My sister's murder was anything but a professional hit. It was—" *Not quick, not painless.*

"I know." He was quiet for a moment. "But think about this. Both Tony and Lily were given knockout drugs. After the murder, Tony's truck was driven across a railroad track to make it look like a murder–suicide attempt. He was found unresponsive inside with the murder weapon in the back of his vehicle. On the surface, it seemed like a crime of passion, but that many steps took planning and coordination."

Veda remained incredulous. "Why would the mob come after an eighteen-year-old girl in Milton, Mississippi, of all places? It sounds ridiculous to even say it out loud."

"Maybe they weren't after Lily. Maybe her murder was meant to send a message to Michael Legend."

She considered the possibility for a moment, then shrugged. "I don't buy it."

"I'm not convinced, either," he admitted.

"Then, why did we just have this conversation?"

"Because I thought you had a right to know about Stipes's claim. And because you need to be fully aware of the potential risks before we confront Michael Legend."

"Consider me forewarned." She picked up her coffee and sipped.

Jon did the same, though he hardly seemed aware of his action. He had a look on his face as if he were lost in deep thought. "I don't think Lily's death was a revenge killing or a professional hit, but I do think it's possible or even probable that she was murdered to keep her from talking."

"About the affair?"

He nodded. "Michael Legend is the most likely suspect at the moment. And Tony was framed because he was the most likely suspect at the time of the murder. The killer knew if he planted enough evidence, the local police would stop looking." His tone turned almost apologetic. "This whole conversation is guesswork. But I wanted you to know everything I know before I drag you into something we may both end up regretting."

Was he talking about a visit to Michael Legend or something more personal?

"I'm not afraid," she said stubbornly.

"I know. That's why I am."

He was looking at her in that way again, as if he couldn't quite figure out how the two of them had ended up alone in her backyard after all these years. She knew that feeling well. Fate could play some interesting tricks. Here she sat in her pajamas calmly discussing mob hits with the man who had once accused her of lying on the witness stand. But that encounter outside the courtroom was starting to dim. She had an inkling now of what he'd been going through.

His voice dropped as his gaze deepened. "Should we talk about this?"

The question startled her, but she didn't pretend to misunderstand him. "At some point, yes, but not now. You just lost your brother. You haven't even laid him to rest yet. It's only human to want a distraction."

His blue eyes glinted in the morning light. "You think that's all this is? A distraction?"

"I don't know. I do know now is not the time to make any important decisions, let alone commitments. Your emotions and judgment are unreliable. If you still feel the same way six months down the road, then we can talk."

"Six months is a long time." He smiled but there was sadness in his eyes and maybe a hint of resignation that something was over before it had begun.

"The experts would probably say a year, but..." she smiled back "...I'm only human, too."

He took her hand, lightly toying with her fingers. "You said you're only here temporarily. What happens if I still feel the same in six months but you're already gone?"

"Then, come and find me."

LATER THAT MORNING, Jon came by to pick Veda up for the hour and a half drive to Biloxi. She'd been to the resort town many times as a kid. Before her dad died, he would load the family up in his big SUV for a day at the beach. Sometimes they would rent a house and stay for a long weekend. Veda and Lily would usually get the second bedroom and the boys would camp out on the living room floor. Sometimes she and her sister would slip out of their room in the middle of the night and the four siblings would tell ghost stories until all hours. They would spend the next day lazing on the beach, swimming and building sandcastles.

When Veda looked back on the carefree days of her early childhood, it was like remembering a dream, hazy and idyllic. Then in the blink of an eye, her dad was gone, and all of their lives had changed. Her mother had found a full-time job as a bookkeeper, and she sometimes worked retail on weekends for extra cash. A life insurance policy had provided a cushion, but her mom insisted that money was only to be used for emergencies and education, not for luxuries like family vacations. Her mother's frugality had enabled Veda to graduate medical school with manageable student loans instead of crushing debt, and she would always be thankful for that. She was grateful to her mother for a lot of things. The heart attack six months ago had made her realize just how much she needed her family.

She felt Jon's hand on hers, and she turned in surprise.

"You were deep in thought just now." He removed his hand as if she might take offense at the intimacy. She didn't.

"I was thinking about my dad. He used to take us to the beach a few times every summer. He and my mom would sit under a big umbrella holding hands while we swam and played in the sand. Even after four kids, they were still so much in love." She sighed wistfully. "At the end of the day, we'd head back home, worn-out and sunburned. And just when we were all about to doze off, Dad would stop to buy us ice cream."

Jon smiled. "My experiences in Biloxi were a little different. My buddies and I would drive down for spring break every year. It was a wild time. Tony talked me into letting him come with us once. Two days in, I had to take him back home to be with Lily. They were inseparable back then. It was a little annoying at times."

"It always comes back to them, doesn't it?" Veda leaned her head against the seat. "In some ways, it feels as if we're still living in their shadows." She turned to study his profile. "I didn't mean that the way it must have sounded."

"I know what you mean. Their lives were cut short. It's hard to move on until we know the truth."

"Seventeen years is a long time to put your life on hold," she said.

"I didn't feel I had a choice. I'm sure you didn't, either." He turned and met her gaze. "Let's just get through the next few days and see what happens."

Rather than taking comfort in his measured response, Veda felt a sinking sensation in the pit of her stomach. His words sounded ominous, almost as if he had already dismissed the idea of a personal relationship. What had made him change his mind since their conversation in her backyard earlier that morning? And did it really matter? For all intents and purposes, they barely knew each other. It only seemed as if they had a connection because of a shared tragedy.

She turned her head to the window, trying not to think too hard about the situation. As Jon said, they needed to get through the next few days. Then she would decide about her future, regardless of what happened between her and Jon Redmond.

Once they neared the coast, she lowered the window to enjoy the salt air. The breeze whipping through her hair brought back those nostalgic memories from her childhood. Lily holding her hand as they ran squealing into the surf. Lily floating beside her gazing up at the sky. Lily sunburned and happy and laughing into the wind.

Those were the images Veda wanted to hold onto forever.

MICHAEL LEGEND LIVED on the west side of town in a three-story home shaded by live oaks. Palm trees and hibiscus bushes lined a brick driveway that wound around to the front of the house, where an ornate staircase led up to a second-story entrance. The front landscaping was lush and immaculate, and the back of the house would have sweeping views of the gulf.

No wonder he didn't want to give all this up over an affair with a student, Veda thought as they made their way up the steps to the covered veranda. She could hear the surf, could imagine all too easily her sister's laughter in the sea breeze that rustled the palmettos.

Jon rang the bell, and Veda gave him an anxious look as they waited. A woman wearing a white tennis skirt and sleeveless top answered the door. She was tanned, toned and attractive in the way that middle-aged women of means always seemed to be. Her blond hair was pulled back in a sleek ponytail that set off her high cheekbones and the diamond studs that twinkled in her lobes.

She gazed back at them expectantly. "May I help you?" she asked in a cultured drawl.

"My name is Jon Redmond. I'm with the Webber County District Attorney's Office." He pulled a card from his jacket pocket and handed it to her. "My associate and I would like to speak to Mr. Legend. Is he home?"

She said coolly, "May I inquire as to what business the Webber County DA's Office has with my husband? The last time I checked, we live in Harrison County. And the DA is a personal friend of ours."

Dropping names already, Veda thought.

"We just have a few questions," Jon persisted. "Is he home?"

"Who is it, Kathryn?" a voice called from the foyer. A second later, a man wearing crisp chinos and a knit pullover appeared behind the woman. He looked to be in his late forties, handsome and fit with crinkles around his eyes and silver threads at his temples. Veda recognized him immediately from the photograph in her sister's secret stash and from his time at Milton High School. She studied him covertly, taking in his expensive yet casual attire, the way he carried himself, the slight lift of one eyebrow as his gaze shifted from Jon to Veda and lingered.

He placed his hands protectively on his wife's shoulders as she turned to gaze up at him. "They're with the Webber County DA's Office." She handed him the card that Jon had presented to her.

"Are you Mr. Legend?" Jon asked. "Michael Legend?"

He glanced up from the card. "I am. What's this about?"

"We're investigating a possible connection between a recent homicide and one that occurred seventeen years ago," Jon explained. "We have a few questions about your time as a guidance counselor at Milton High School. Is now a good time?"

"Homicides?" Kathryn Legend stared back at Jon as if he'd taken leave of his senses. Then her gaze moved to Veda. Something that might have been recognition—or anger—flickered in her eyes. "There must be some mistake."

"No mistake, but the questions are strictly routine," Jon explained. "We'll only take a few minutes of your time."

Kathryn turned and placed her hand on her husband's arm. "Should I call Harry?"

"That won't be necessary. You heard what the man said. The questions are routine." Legend patted her hand. "Everything is fine. You go on without me."

She didn't look convinced. "Are you sure?"

He kissed her forehead. "Yes, absolutely. I'll take care of this matter and meet you at the club for lunch."

She reluctantly turned to disappear back into the house, but not before glancing over her shoulder at Veda.

Legend studied the business card. "You're Jon Redmond?"

"Yes."

"So you're not just *with* the DA's office. You're the district attorney for Webber County."

"Correct."

"Redmond." He repeated the name as if it had struck a chord. "Any relation to Tony Redmond?"

The question must have surprised Jon, but he didn't outwardly react. "He was my brother."

"I thought that might be the case." He gave Jon a sympathetic nod. "My condolences. I read about your brother's death in the paper. The name caught my attention because I remembered a Tony Redmond from my time at Milton High school. He was a football star. Very charismatic, as I recall." His gaze shifted to Veda. "I'm sorry. I didn't catch your name."

"Veda Campion."

He looked startled. "Campion?"

She wanted to be gratified by his reaction, but coming face-to-face with the man who had seduced her sister— possibly even killed her—and keeping her cool was a lot harder than she imagined. "I'm Lily Campion's sister. She was a senior the year you were at Milton High School."

"Yes, I remember her as well. She was an extraordinary young woman." For a moment, he seemed at a loss. "I must say, I would never have expected to find the two of you together at my door. Am I to understand that you're also with the DA's office?"

"I'm a forensic pathologist," Veda told him. "Until a couple of days ago, I was the acting coroner for Webber County."

"Impressive, though hardly surprising," he said with a smile. "I remember you as well. You showed the same promise as your sister."

He was good, Veda thought. Agreeable and charming with only a hint of the arrogance she remembered.

"Perhaps you'd both better come inside." He scanned the scenery behind them as if worried someone walking by might see them on his doorstep.

He led them down a wide hallway to a set of heavy doors which he slid apart and then gestured for them to enter. Closing the doors, he moved around the office and motioned to the chairs across from a large desk. "Please, have a seat." He sat down behind the desk and folded his hands on the surface. "I'm curious. How did you know you would find me at home this morning? I'm usually at work this time of day."

"I called your office," Jon said candidly. "Your assistant said you were taking some time off and wouldn't be available until Friday."

"And you took that as your cue to show up at my house unannounced?"

"As I said, we won't take much of your time."

Legend sat back in his chair, eyeing them across his desk. He didn't look nervous or angry. He seemed more bemused than anything else. "You said you're investigating two homicides that were committed seventeen years apart. I take it you were referring to your brother and Lily Campion?"

"Yes."

"And you think there's a connection that has something to do with my time at Milton High School? I was only there a year."

"You were the guidance counselor, which means you must have spoken to any number of students. Maybe you noticed a pattern of behavior. We're hoping one of our questions may trigger a memory."

He still looked perplexed. "Wasn't your brother convicted of Lily's murder?"

"If you read about his death in the paper, then you probably also know that his conviction was recently overturned."

"Because of prosecutorial misconduct. It wasn't an exoneration."

He seemed well-informed on Tony Redmond's history, Veda noted.

"Let's get back to your time as a guidance counselor," Jon said. "How well did you know Lily Campion?"

He fiddled with a pen on his desk. "As well as I knew any of the students, I suppose. She worked in the office a few hours a week, so perhaps a little better than most."

"What was your impression of her?"

"She was bright, attractive, hardworking. And troubled." He glanced at Veda. "But I'm sure you already know that." He returned his focus to Jon. "I still don't understand why you think any of this is helpful or relevant. And I would imagine asking these kinds of questions brings up a lot of painful memories for her sister."

"Don't worry about me," Veda assured him.

"Just bear with us a little longer," Jon added. "You said Lily was *troubled*. Can you elaborate?"

"She suffered from depression and mood swings. Again, something her family would have noticed as well. She had a hard time opening up to people, but after a while she did tell me a little about her background. Something traumatic happened to her as a child."

"Our father died in a car crash," Veda explained. "He and Lily were very close."

"She mentioned the accident once. Even years later, she had a difficult time talking about it. She seemed completely devastated by the loss. I got the sense that she blamed herself for his death. I don't believe she ever got over it."

Veda leaned in. "Why do you think she blamed herself?"

He gave her a brief, humorless smile. "Surely you would know that better than I."

She'd taken control of the interview without really meaning to, but Jon seemed content to sit quietly and allow her to proceed as she saw fit. "You said Lily had a hard time opening up. She did. Especially to her family. She was very private. Perhaps even secretive. I loved my sister, but in some ways, I feel as if I never really knew her. If there is anything you can tell me about her, about her emotional state during those last few months, I would be grateful."

She had his attention now. Despite his outward reluctance, he seemed intrigued by her request. "She never said why she blamed herself, but my guess is they argued before he died. She was left in an emotional limbo, never able to make things right. She told me once that she had gaps in her memory before and after the accident. The only thing she could remember clearly was her uncle waking her up in the middle of the night to tell her the news about her parents."

"I remember that, too." Veda had rarely shared her memories of that terrible night. She still found it difficult, but something about Legend's expression and body language when he spoke about Lily suggested he was more absorbed in the conversation than he pretended to be. If she could keep him engrossed, perhaps he'd let something important slip about his relationship with her sister.

"That must have been a traumatic time for all of you," he said.

"Yes, but it hit Lily especially hard. After my uncle woke us up, he had us come downstairs to the living room where he told us about the accident together. The first thing he did was assure us that our mother was fine. She had to spend the night in the hospital, but she would be home in a day or two. But Dad...he didn't make it."

"I'm sorry."

She wasn't sure if the murmured condolence had come from Michael Legend or from Jon.

"How old were you when this happened?"

What he really wanted to know was Lily's age, Veda thought.

"I was eight at the time. Lily was ten. My five-year-old brother and I burst into uncontrollable tears. I'm not sure he even comprehended what had happened, but he knew we were all distressed. My older brother came and sat between us. He put his arms around us and told us everything would be all right. He would take care of us. But Lily just sat there alone, stoic and tearless. It was almost as if she didn't hear a word our uncle said until he tried to comfort her. Then she started screaming and didn't stop until he called a local doctor who came and gave her a sedative."

"Pharmaceuticals might account for the gaps in her memory," Legend mused.

Jon still said nothing, but she could feel his gaze on her. She hadn't meant to bare her soul, only to share enough to keep Michael Legend engaged and off guard. But once the words started to flow, she couldn't get them out quickly enough. Maybe Lily wasn't the only one who had carried the burden of that night quietly.

"Veda—" Jon said her name so softly she wondered if she had imagined his voice. Her hand had been gripping the chair arm. She lifted a finger to signal she was okay.

She refocused on Legend. "Did Lily tell you she was planning to run away with someone after graduation?"

He frowned. "Not that I recall. By *someone*, do you mean her boyfriend?"

"I don't mean Tony Redmond. I testified at his trial that she was seeing someone behind his back. She never told me his name, and he never came forward." She paused. "Did she ever mention a name to you, even in passing? Did she ever express interest in anyone other than Tony?"

He took a long moment to answer as if sensing a trap. "We weren't that close."

"Close enough that she told you about our father's death and the guilt she felt afterward."

"That was different."

Jon took over the questioning. "Were you and Lily romantically involved?"

Michael Legend drew a sharp breath, his dark eyes snapping with anger and perhaps a hint of fear, Veda thought.

"You have some nerve, coming into my home and making such a monstrous accusation."

"It's not an accusation," Jon said. "Just a simple question."

His expression hardened. "Then, let me make one thing perfectly clear to you. My wife and I were married during the first semester of that school year. We were deeply committed to one another, but even if I'd been single, that is a line I would never have crossed with a student."

"How do you explain these?" Veda set the stack of letters on his desk, followed by the photo.

He examined the image and shrugged. "I've never seen that photograph in my life. I have no idea when or where it was taken." He picked up the letters and thumbed through the envelopes. "What are these?"

"Love letters to my sister," Veda told him.

He tossed them onto the desk with careless disregard. "They're not from me. That's not even my handwriting."

"Would you be willing to provide a sample for comparison?" Jon asked.

"No, I would not. You're lucky I've been willing to sit here for as long as I have, but my patience is wearing thin."

Veda retrieved the stack from his desk and removed the breakup letter. She took out the single page and read some of the lines aloud. *"Stop calling me. Stop writing to me. Stop watching my house. If you ever come near my property again, you'll find out just how angry I can get."* She glanced up. "You didn't write that?"

He looked momentarily stunned. Then he quickly recovered and nodded to the letter in her hand. "May I?" She handed the page back to him, and he quickly scanned the lines. Then he folded the paper and returned it to Veda. "I didn't write that letter—any of these letters—but I think I know who did."

Veda found herself leaning forward in her chair yet again. "Who?"

"I think Lily wrote them."

Now it was Veda who sat stunned. She felt simultaneously outraged and shattered on her sister's behalf. She told herself he would say anything to keep his secret, but a voice in her head was already starting to whisper. *What if he's right?*

She exchanged a glance with Jon.

He said to Legend, "Why do you think Lily wrote them?"

His anger had evaporated, and he gave Veda a concerned look. "This may be difficult for you to hear. I didn't write that letter, but I once said those very words to her."

"Why?"

He rubbed a hand over his eyes. "I never suspected she had feelings for me—romantic feelings—until the end of the school year. Then she started leaving anonymous notes in my office. Sometimes little gifts. She even sent letters to my house. She disguised her handwriting so that it took me a while to figure out who they were from. When I confronted her, she readily owned up to it. She said she was in love with me and had been for months."

"And you never had an inkling?" Veda asked.

"I was in love with my wife. The thought never crossed my mind. But Lily insisted that she could tell I felt the same way but couldn't admit it because I didn't want Kathryn to get hurt. I tried to let her down gently, but the more I rebuffed her affection, the more desperate she became. She began leaving explicit voice mail messages. Sometimes, I would see her parked across the street from my house. She even broke in once." He nodded to the letter. "It's true I said those things to her, but I didn't write that letter. I certainly never wrote her any love letters."

"Did you report the break-in to the police?" Jon asked.

"No. I didn't have proof it was her, and I just wanted the situation to go away. I had already decided against renewing my contract for the following school year. I hoped once the semester ended, things would blow over."

"Did you tell anyone else about her behavior?" Jon asked.

"My wife knew."

"Did she and Lily ever have words?"

"Kathryn wanted to confront her, but I told her we were dealing with a very troubled individual. The last thing we needed to do was antagonize her. Eventually the phone calls stopped. Sometime later, I heard she was dead. Murdered." He closed his eyes on a deep sigh. "As much trouble as she caused me, I would never have wished something so tragic on her and her family"

"Why didn't you come forward at the time of her murder?" Jon asked.

He made a helpless gesture with his hand. "Why would I? I had nothing useful to offer the police, and I was about to embark on a new career. Kathryn and I had our whole lives ahead of us. I wanted to put all that unpleasantness behind us. Besides, Lily's family had been through enough. Why inflict more pain?" He shoved back his chair and stood, signaling an end to the meeting. "I've told you everything I remember. If you'll excuse me, I have a lunch date with my wife."

Jon and Veda rose, too. "Just one more question," he said. "Did my brother come to see you after he got out of prison?"

"He most certainly did not. The last time I saw him was seventeen years ago."

"You're sure about that?"

Michael Legend nodded to the door. "You can show yourselves out. Should either of you have further questions, you can contact me through my attorney."

Chapter Eleven

"You're awfully quiet," Jon observed a few minutes later when they were headed back home. He'd remained silent, too, concentrating on his driving until they were well away from Beach Boulevard. Then he turned to search her profile. She was staring straight ahead, hands clasped in her lap. The meeting with Michael Legend had left a sour taste in his mouth. He could only imagine what she must be feeling. "Do you want to talk about it?"

She sighed and let her head drop to the back of the seat. "I think I'm still in shock. I may need a little more time to process what he said about Lily."

"Regarding the letters?"

Her head came up, and he heard a tremor of anger in her voice. "He made her sound like a stalker. Like someone so far removed from reality that she wrote letters to herself and pretended they were from him. Then she broke into his home?" She closed her eyes on a shudder. "I'll be the first to admit that my sister had her emotional ups and downs, but she wasn't deranged."

"Just because he said it doesn't mean it's true," Jon reminded her. "For all we know he was covering his tracks."

She turned to meet his gaze. "But what if he's right?

What if Lily did write those letters? What if the affair was only in her imagination? Where does that leave us?"

"It leaves us exactly where we were before we talked to Michael Legend," he said. "As far as I'm concerned, he's still our lead suspect. Think about it. He knew those letters were out there and that they might eventually surface. He's had seventeen years to come up with a plausible story. Don't take anything he said at face value."

"But why would he write them in the first place? If he was so desperate to keep their relationship a secret, why take the risk?"

"Because the risk of getting caught was part of the thrill." Jon rubbed the back of his neck. "I've dealt with guys like that for most of my career. Their egos almost always trip them up. He loved having the adoration of someone like Lily until she started showing up at his house. He knew if his wife found out about the affair, the lucrative position he had lined up at his father-in-law's company would vanish. He had to do something drastic."

"That's all well and good," Veda said, "but we still don't have any proof. And from where I was sitting, we didn't exactly rattle his cage."

"We'll see." He stopped for a traffic light and scanned their surroundings. Traffic had thinned as they approached the outskirts of town. Businesses dwindled, giving way to litter-strewn ditches and weedy parking lots. He waited for the light to change before he tentatively broached another subject. "That must have been hard for you, recounting the night your dad died to the man who may have murdered your sister. I know what you were trying to do, but you didn't have to open yourself up like that. Not to him."

Veda shrugged. "I wanted to keep him engaged. Despite what he said, I had the impression he enjoyed talking about Lily."

Jon kept his eyes on the road, but he could glimpse her in his periphery. She still sat staring straight ahead, her blond hair loose and wavy about her shoulders, her hazel eyes shadowed and troubled. In some ways, it still seemed strange that they should find themselves working together so closely, yet he couldn't imagine doing this without her. Maybe she was right. Maybe it was too soon to trust his judgment, let alone make any life-altering decisions. But if his brother's death had taught him anything, aside from the unfairness of life, it was that even a moment of happiness was worth fighting for.

He gave her a sidelong glance. "You said Marcus is the one who told you about your parents' accident. You don't have to talk about it if you don't want to," he was quick to add.

"I don't mind talking about it to you. My dad had gone to Tennessee to get my mom. My grandmother had fallen ill, and my mom was taking care of her. She and my dad were supposed to drive back the following day, but my mom said she had the strongest feeling they needed to get home that night. My dad had arranged for a neighbor to come over and stay with us until they got back. Marcus sent her home so that he could tell us the news himself."

"I'm sorry," Jon said. "I know what it's like to lose a parent at a young age. My dad was sick for a long time, so his death didn't come as a shock. But it leaves a void in your life, no matter your age or the circumstances."

"That goes for any loved one," she said. "This must be even harder for you. You've barely taken the time to grieve."

"It helps to have something to focus on. Besides, finding

Tony's killer is all that matters to me right now." Sooner or later his brother's death would hit him hard. He knew that. Right now, though, he needed to stay motivated.

He glanced in the rearview and swore.

"What's wrong?"

A police cruiser with flashing blue lights had come out of nowhere to tail them. At first, Jon thought the driver might pass him, but then the siren sounded. "We're being pulled over."

Veda twisted around to stare out the back window. "Were you speeding?"

"Not by much. Not enough to get stopped." He slowed until he found a safe place to pull over. They were still in the area of town where the landscape looked more rural than urban. Little to no traffic. Trees and vines encroaching on deserted buildings. They may as well have been in the middle of nowhere.

Jon had a bad feeling about the stop. "Just stay calm," he told Veda.

She whirled to face him. "Why wouldn't I stay calm? This is just a routine traffic stop, right?"

"I don't know." He lowered his window and killed the engine.

She said in alarm, "What do you mean you don't know? What do you think is going on?"

"We'll soon find out. Whatever happens, just keep a cool head and do what they say." He reached across her legs to retrieve his registration and proof of insurance from the glove box.

The police car pulled up behind them. The siren was shut off, but the blue lights kept flashing. No one got out of the car.

Veda craned back around. "What are they doing?"

"Probably running my plates."

"You don't have any outstanding warrants, do you?" She was only half-joking.

"That would be frowned upon in my line of work." He removed his driver's license from his wallet and waited, his gaze riveted on the rearview mirror.

Veda said uneasily, "I don't like this. Did you happen to notice there's no other traffic on the road?"

"We're a few blocks over from a busy intersection. We'll be fine." He hoped he sounded more encouraging than he actually felt. He told himself it was probably just a speed trap. A couple of patrol cops looking to make their monthly quota.

Another few minutes went by before two officers got out of the cruiser and sauntered toward the car. Jon could hear the sputter of their radios as he tracked their progress in the rearview. A few feet from his car, they split up. One stayed behind the vehicle while the other approached his lowered window.

He kept his hands on the wheel until the officer was beside him, and then he glanced up. "What's the problem, Officer?"

"License, registration and proof of insurance."

Jon handed him the paperwork and returned his hands to the steering wheel.

"Is this still your current address?" He held up the license and squinted at Jon through the window.

"Yes."

"You're from Milton. That's up in Webber County. The DA over there is named Redmond. You wouldn't happen to know him, would you?"

"I'm Jon Redmond."

He nodded. "I figured as much. Just to be clear, this is Harrison County, so your credentials in Webber County don't mean a lot down here."

Jon kept his voice carefully neutral. "I understand, but you haven't told me why you pulled me over."

"You were weaving across the center line. You haven't been drinking, have you?" He bent to glance in the window at Veda.

"I haven't been drinking." And he knew damn well he hadn't been weaving across the center line.

"Would you mind stepping out of the car?"

Jon's natural inclination was to resist even though he knew better. "Is that really necessary?"

The officer stepped back from the window and placed a hand on his weapon. "Sir, step out of the car now, and keep your hands where I can see them."

The situation had escalated quickly. Too quickly. Jon was getting the impression this was all a setup. It wasn't a coincidence that the officer had recognized his name. He flashed a warning look to Veda as he opened the car door. Her eyes were wide with apprehension, but she didn't appear panicked.

The second officer came around to the passenger side. He opened the door and motioned for her to get out. Jon heard him tell her to stay put. Meanwhile, the first officer instructed him to turn and face the vehicle.

"I don't consent to a search," he said.

"Too bad." The officer grabbed him from behind, twisted his arm back and slammed him against the car. Jon wasn't hurt, but his blood had started to boil. He counted to ten as his legs were kicked apart and the officer proceeded to pat him down. "Just keep your mouth shut, do as we say, and you'll be on your way soon enough. Now." He took a step back. "We're going to need you to open the trunk."

Jon glanced over his shoulder. "Not without a warrant."

"We don't need a warrant when we have probable cause."

"Of what?" he demanded.

"I *said* open the damn trunk." The officer yanked both Jon's arms behind him. Searing pain shot up his biceps and across his shoulder blades. "Don't resist," he warned while he slapped on the cuffs. "Where's the key?"

"Right pocket."

Jon glanced at Veda across the top of the car and mouthed *Are you okay?*

She nodded and gave him a tentative smile to reassure him.

The officer fished out the fob and clicked open the trunk. He moved to the rear of the vehicle to search the space while the second officer rifled through the glove box and console compartment before checking under the floor mats and beneath the seats. Jon kept an eye out as best he could in case they tried to plant something in the car.

When they were finished, he half expected one of them to present a bag of crystal meth and then haul him off to jail. Instead, the officer closed the trunk and came back around to remove the cuffs.

"Sorry for the inconvenience." His tone had completely changed. "We got a tip from a concerned citizen that a car matching this description might be transporting drugs across state lines. Better safe than sorry."

Jon rubbed his wrists. "Who was the concerned citizen?"

The officer gave him back the key fob. "You folks have a good day, now."

They returned to the cruiser, and Jon and Veda climbed back into the car. She gave him a nervous look before turning to glance out the back window. "What was that all about?"

"I think we were just warned," he said.

Her hand flew to her chest. "You think Michael Legend sent them?"

"Let's just say his connection to the Dixie Mafia sounds a little more plausible than it did a few hours ago."

She picked up her purse from the floor and opened the clasp. "I thought certain they were going to plant drugs on us." She rummaged through her belongings.

"The same notion crossed my mind." He pressed the starter button and pulled away from the curb. The cruiser remained parked as if waiting for him to make a wrong move.

"Jon."

"What is it?"

She looked up, stricken. "The letters are gone."

He kept an eye on the rearview. "Are you sure? Could they have fallen out when you climbed out of the car?"

"No. I put them in a zippered compartment in my bag." She kept digging. "The photograph is missing, too."

"I guess we rattled a cage after all."

"It seems as though we did," she agreed. "Good thing I scanned everything to my computer last night before I went to bed."

"Send me a copy as soon as we get home."

She nodded. "You know what this means, don't you? He was lying about the letters. Why else would he go to such lengths to get them back?"

"Assuming he's the one who sent the cops to retrieve them."

Her head came up as her eyes widened. "Who else could it be?"

"Think about it for a minute."

She bit her lip in consternation. "He said his wife knew about the affair."

He nodded.

She dropped her purse to the floor and sat back against the seat. "That makes sense. She's the one with the connections. Maybe it was my imagination, but I could have sworn she recognized me."

Jon interjected a note of caution. "I saw that look, too, but let's not jump to any conclusions. We go slow and think it through, remember? I know how you feel, but promise me you won't do anything rash."

"Like what?"

"Like confront Kathryn Legend." He glanced at her again. "Don't tell me that isn't going through your mind right now."

"It is, but I wouldn't do anything without telling you first. We're in this together. You wouldn't go behind my back, either, would you? We share everything, right?"

"Right." He hoped she hadn't noticed the slight hesitation before he answered.

A DARK SUV was parked at the curb in front of Veda's house when they got home. She recognized the vehicle immediately.

"Were you expecting company?" Jon pulled into the driveway and parked.

"That's Nate. What's he doing here in the middle of the day?" she mused worriedly.

"No jumping to conclusions, remember?"

But Veda was already out of the car. Her brother rose from the porch swing and came down the steps to meet her on the walkway. "Where have you been? I've been waiting here for close to an hour."

She immediately bristled at his accusing tone. Her older brother always had a way of putting her on the defensive. "How is that my fault? Why didn't you call first?"

"I wanted to talk to you in person." His gaze moved past her to Jon, who lingered at his open car door. His mouth thinned as he returned his focus to his sister. "What's he doing here?"

"We'll talk about that later," she said. "Why were you waiting for me?"

His voice lowered. "This is a discussion we need to have in private."

Alarm shot up her spine. "Why? What's going on? Is it Mom?"

"It's not Mom." His gaze moved back to Jon. "I take it he didn't see fit to tell you."

"Tell me what? Nate, what's going on? Just say it, for God's sake."

"Owen has been arrested."

VEDA SPENT THE rest of the day with her family. Nate was allowed to see Owen that afternoon and reported that their brother was handling the situation as well as could be expected, but Veda worried. The murder weapon had been found in a dumpster near Owen's apartment. That was new information, and coupled with the very public threat—not to mention the vicious fight—it didn't look good. Owen had no alibi for the time in question and a very long history of animosity toward the victim. The evidence against him was circumstantial, but innocent people had been convicted on less.

Nate had already contacted an attorney while Veda and her mother started making arrangements for bail money once Owen was arraigned. Everything that could be done was being done, but the preparations did little to ease Veda's mind. A question kept intruding. Had Jon known that the arrest was forthcoming? Maybe that explained the change in his attitude she'd sensed from the time they'd had coffee in her backyard to their subsequent trip to Biloxi. *Let's just get through the next few days*, he'd said. Had he known what was coming?

By the time Nate dropped her off at her house, she was exhausted and emotionally drained. She wanted nothing so much as a long shower, a glass of wine and hours of sleep.

But a little while later, she was still wide-awake, sitting alone at the breakfast table sipping wine and eating chips when she heard a car pull up outside. She went through the house and glanced out the front window. Jon was just coming up the walkway. She drew open the door and stepped out on the dark porch.

"Jon, it's late. It's been a long day, and I was just going to bed. Can this wait?"

"I won't keep you." He moved across the porch. "I wanted to make sure you're okay."

She wrapped her arms around her middle. "My brother was arrested for murder today, and he's currently sitting in the county jail. I'm not okay."

"Is there anything I can do?"

"Can you get him out?"

"I can't do that," he said. "But I can walk you through

what to expect over the next few days. Maybe that will help ease your mind."

"Or make things worse." She couldn't stop shivering all of a sudden. "I need to ask you a question. Did you know Owen was going to be arrested when you came here this morning?"

"I didn't know for certain, but I knew it was a possibility. We talked about that, remember?"

"Would you have told me if you did know?"

He looked her straight in the eyes. "I can't answer that. You're asking me about a hypothetical. All I can say is it would depend on the circumstances."

She leaned back against the doorframe and closed her eyes briefly. "I'm getting a sense of what it must have been like for your family. For you. This feeling of helplessness and anger and disbelief. And loneliness. God, it's so lonely on this side."

"I know."

"It's strange, isn't it? How our roles have suddenly reversed?"

"With one important distinction." His gaze on her even in the dark was intense. "Owen hasn't been convicted of anything yet. There's still time to prove his innocence."

She clung to his words. "He didn't do it," she said fiercely.

"And I'll do everything I can to help you prove that. But you should know my official role is limited. I'm recused from the case."

"You still have contacts, though."

He answered carefully. "Some."

"After I left the crime scene the other night, I went to Owen's apartment. I saw a dark sedan parked across the street. I had the notion that someone may have been watching his apartment. The car even followed me when I left. Do you think the killer planted the gun in the dumpster that night?"

"It's possible. Have you told the police?"

"I told Detective Calloway about it today. But I don't know how much it will help. I didn't get a license plate number. I'm not even sure of the make or model."

"Why didn't you say anything before now?"

"I know this sounds lame, but it slipped my mind." She hesitated. "You believe me, don't you?"

"I believe you."

She drew a deep breath and released it. "I'm sorry."

"For what?"

"For not believing you back then."

"The circumstances are different. You had every reason to believe Tony did it. I don't fault you for that." He paused as their gazes clung in the dark. "Veda." The way he said her name made her heart thud. "I know the other side is lonely, but you're not alone. You have your family, and you have me."

She took his hand and drew him inside. He closed the door and turned. She stood in her tiny foyer, needing his arms around her more than she had ever needed anything in her life. For comfort, yes. But for so much more.

He closed the distance between them and wrapped his arms around her, lifting her up to his kiss. She cupped his face and kissed him back, then threaded her fingers through his hair. Her pajamas were thin cotton, practically nonexistent. She could feel the warmth of his hands on her back, then her breasts. She pulled away and ripped off her top. Then they were kissing again, through the foyer, across the living room and down the short hallway to her bedroom.

Somewhere along the way, he lost his shirt and shoes. They stood at the side of the bed and finished undressing. When they finally crawled between the cool sheets, he moved on top of her, propping himself on one arm as he smoothed back her hair.

"This isn't exactly taking our time and thinking things through," he said.

"I don't care."

"Me, either."

The talk died away to sighs and whispers. Their fingers intertwined as their bodies came together. She didn't think about his family or hers. She didn't think about the past or the future. At that very moment, she wanted to feel, not think.

Her breath quickened, and she held on tightly as her body began to shudder.

SOMETIME LATER, Veda walked Jon to the door. He was fully dressed. She was back in her pajamas. Her hair was uncombed, but she didn't care. His kiss was far from gentle, and yet it was. "Try to get some rest. You've a long day ahead of you tomorrow."

"I don't want to think about that right now."

"Then, don't. Get some sleep."

"Jon." She wrapped her arms around him and held on tightly. He hugged her back. Neither of them said anything for the longest moment. They just stood there embracing as the world rushed in on them. Veda had never experienced anything so intimate in her life.

Chapter Twelve

The next morning, Veda was up early, showered, dressed and having her first cup of coffee on the front porch when Nate called. "I don't want to alarm you," he said, which of course immediately alarmed her.

"What's wrong?"

"This time it is Mom. We're at the hospital. She's okay," he quickly added. "I went by her house this morning to check on her. She was having chest pains. I brought her to the ER, and the doctor is in with her now. He says she'll be fine. It wasn't a heart attack. Probably a panic attack, but he wants to keep her in the hospital for a day or two to monitor her blood pressure."

Veda was already on her feet and rushing back inside for her keys. "Why didn't you call me sooner?"

"I'm calling you now. I've arranged to see Owen this morning. Can you come stay with Mom?"

"I'll be there in fifteen minutes. Ten if I don't catch any lights."

She was there in eight. Her mother was still in the ER awaiting a room. She reached for Veda's hand when she walked through the door. "I told Nate not to call you."

"Why?"

"I didn't want to worry you. The doctor says I'll be fine."

"He also wants to keep you here for a couple of days. Just to be on the safe side."

Her grip tightened on Veda's fingers. "I can't stay here. I need to be with Owen."

"Nate is with Owen," Veda reassured her. "You won't be able to see him until after the arraignment, anyway. Mom, just try to rest. That's the best thing you can do for Owen at the moment."

She said on a tremulous sigh, "I feel like I've let you kids down."

"That's not true. You've been both mother and father to us. We couldn't have asked for a better parent."

Tears filled her mother's eyes. "I couldn't protect Lily. Now I can't protect Owen."

"Owen will be fine. He's innocent. We're going to prove that." Veda perched on the edge of the bed, still clinging to her mother's hand. "Jon has a theory. Don't be upset," she was quick to add. "Just hear me out. He thinks the same person who killed Lily also killed Tony. That person wasn't Owen."

"It's true, then." Her mother's voice dropped. "You've been seeing Jon Redmond. I couldn't believe it when Marcus told me."

Veda was quick to his defense. "Jon did nothing that any of us wouldn't do for Owen."

"Owen is innocent," her mother insisted.

"And Jon has always believed Tony was innocent."

"Do you?"

"That's a hard question for me to answer," Veda admitted. "What did Marcus say to you after I left yesterday?"

"He said you've been asking questions about Lily's personal belongings, that you've been looking for her diary."

"Did she have a diary?"

"Why does that matter now?" Her mother looked agitated all of a sudden.

Veda patted her hand. "It doesn't matter. All that matters is that you stay calm and get some rest. Let's talk about something else."

"I can't think about anything but Owen."

"I promise Owen will be fine. He's got Nate looking out for him." He had Jon Redmond, too, but her mom wouldn't want to hear that at the moment.

It was a couple of hours before they came to take her upstairs. Once she was settled, Veda pulled a chair up and sat down at her bedside.

"You don't have to hover, Veda. I'm fine."

"I want to be here, Mom."

"Then, make yourself useful and go pick up a few things from the house. If I have to stay here overnight, I at least want my tablet and reading glasses."

"Make me a list," Veda said. "If it'll make you rest easier, I'll go get them right now."

A little while later, she let herself into the house and went straight to the downstairs bedroom. She collected toiletries from the bathroom and her mother's tablet and reading glasses from the nightstand. Then she went through the house and made sure everything was locked up and all the burners were turned off on the stove. She was just about to leave through the front door when she heard a rustling sound upstairs. Faint but unmistakable. That was strange. No one was home. No other vehicle was parked out front. For a moment, the notion went through Veda's head that

Lily's ghost might really be upstairs. Then she chided herself for the fantasy. Maybe a window had been left open.

Even so, she hovered at the foot of the stairs for several moments before she went up. The hair at the back of her neck prickled as she eased down the hallway. She glanced in Lily's room first. Nothing seemed amiss, although she detected the faint scent of…cedarwood?

Her heart started to thud as she backed out of the room and turned down the hallway. The attic door stood ajar.

JANE CAMPION'S HOSPITAL door was open, but Jon knocked and waited in the hallway because he wasn't at all sure he'd be invited inside. She turned her head and visibly started when she saw him. He put up a hand. "I'm sorry. I didn't mean to startle you."

"Did you come to see Veda? She's not here." She sounded more curious than hostile. He was relieved about that. "I sent her home to pick up some of my things. She should be back soon."

"Actually, I came to see you," he said.

"I guess you'd better come in, then." She propped herself up against the pillows and watched with avid eyes as he came into the room and stood at the foot of her bed. "Veda told me about your theory. You think the same person who killed my Lily killed your brother."

"Yes. That's what I think."

"So you don't think Owen is guilty."

"I do not."

Her chin came up. "Do you expect me to say the same about your brother?"

"I don't expect that, no. That'll take some time."

She closed her eyes briefly. "How's your mother holding up? She's been on my mind ever since I heard the news."

"She's doing as well as can be expected. I'll tell her you asked after her."

She gave him a long scrutiny. "But that's not why you're here."

"No." He came around to the side of the bed. "I want you to tell me about the nightmares Lily used to have."

She looked startled. "Why?"

"Because I'm afraid of what they may mean."

SOMETHING TOLD VEDA not to call out or even make a sound. In fact, her every instinct warned her to get out of the house, but instead she found herself climbing the attic stairs slowly. The steps creaked beneath her feet. She paused to listen. The rustling sounded frenzied and determined. She went up quickly, pausing again at the top. Her grandmother's cedar chest was open, the contents strewn about. Her uncle had his back to her frantically rifling through storage boxes, unaware of her presence. Or so it seemed. Then he turned slowly and said her name. "Veda."

If you see him, pretend you don't know.

A shiver went through her as he got to his feet and faced her. He seemed larger than life at that moment. Looming. Menacing. She could imagine him coming through a bedroom window, eyes glowing red, thunder booming behind him.

She tried to act nonchalant, but her heart had started to pound as those terrible images raced through her head. *You did it. It was you.*

"What are you doing up here?" She glanced around at the mess he'd made. "Are you looking for something?"

His pretenses dropped, and he said with a shrug, "I've wondered about what she might have told you. You were very close. If she would have confided in anyone, it would have been you."

Veda swallowed, still thinking she could talk her way out of it. Then something took hold of her, and she said on a near whisper, "You're the bad man she dreamed about. But you didn't just sit on the edge of her bed and watch her sleep. You did something to her."

"I didn't do what you're thinking. God, not that. I just wanted to touch her. Hold her for a moment. She was so beautiful. And mature for her age. You know that's true."

Veda clapped a hand over her mouth to keep from screaming.

He said as if to himself, "I don't know how it happened, what came over me. She promised she wouldn't tell anyone. Not your mom or dad…no one. It was nothing—"

"Nothing!" Veda was trembling so hard she could barely stand. "Don't you dare downplay what you did to her."

"It wasn't like that—"

"Shut up! Don't say another word or I swear—"

"Calm down," he said in a placating tone. "Let me explain."

Bile rose to her throat. She had to choke it back down. "She trusted you. We all trusted you. How could we have been so blind? Those nightmares she had. That was you. She blamed herself for Dad's death because of what you did. She thought she'd done something wrong, but it was *you.*"

He spread his hands in supplication. "You're making it sound so much worse than it was. It only happened once and she forgot about it. I swear she did. I kept my distance, and no one would ever have known. No one would have gotten hurt. We could have gone on with our lives until she met *him*."

"Tony?"

He seemed not to hear her. "She flaunted him in my face. What was I supposed to do? I couldn't let her be with someone like that. He was a married man." His hands clenched in fury. "They thought they were being careful and clever, but I knew. I always knew what she was up to. The drugs. The partying. I went to her and tried to talk sense into her. I said he would end up ruining her life, but she wouldn't listen. She said I'd already done that. *Me*. The person who cared about her more than anything."

Veda's stomach roiled. "You're disgusting."

He went on as if she'd never spoken. "She told me she remembered everything and that if I ever came near her again, she would tell your mother. She would tell everyone. I could kiss my career goodbye. My friends, my family. I'd end up in prison."

Dear God, Veda thought. How could this have happened and no one knew? Guilt washed over her. "You killed her. You killed my sister. Your own flesh and blood." *Not quick, not painless.* "You're a monster."

"No," he said in strange voice. "I'm just a man who had everything to lose."

Veda felt almost numb to his confession. A part of her realized she was in shock. Later, the impact would be profound. "You drugged Tony. You put that knife in his truck. You drove him to the railroad tracks hoping a train would take care of the rest. A murder–suicide made so much sense. But he didn't die. He went to prison instead. And when he got out, he came to find you."

"He said he'd put it all together while he was on the inside. He said he knew what I'd done, and he was going to make me pay." He shrugged. "Big words. He had no proof, but I knew he wouldn't let it go. I followed him to a place out on the highway that night. He never knew what hit him. That should have been the end of it, but then you and Jon started looking for her diary."

"There isn't a diary. There was never a diary. No one would have ever known."

He looked around at the disarray he'd created. "But now you know. It's over, isn't it?"

"It's over."

She turned and started down the stairs, but she'd misjudged what he meant. It wasn't over for him. It was over for her.

He came down the stairs so quickly he caught her by surprise. He grabbed her around the neck and the waist and hauled her back up the steps. Then he flung her to the floor and straddled her, his hands clamping around her throat. She fought him. Hard. To save her own life, yes, but also for Lily. And Tony. For both their families.

"Shush. It's okay. Everything will be okay." She could smell the undertones of cedarwood in his aftershave as she flailed. "They'll just think the door locked behind you. That latch has always been faulty. You had to climb onto the roof to get out. You fell and broke your neck. I'll make sure Dr. Bader confirms cause of death. Your mother will be devastated, but I'll be there for her and your brothers. We'll all move on eventually. It'll be okay."

Veda tore at his hands, clawed her nails across his face. He squeezed tighter, tighter until her breath grew shallow and her struggles less frantic. She was going to die at the hands of Lily's killer. No one would ever know because he was that good at lying. He was that adept at covering his tracks.

"Veda? Are you up there?"

Jon!

She tried to call for help. Nothing came out but a croak.

I don't want to die. I don't want to die.

"Let her go."

His voice came from the top of the stairs. Her uncle's grip loosened. He rose and drew his weapon.

Jon! Jon! She tried to scream a warning, but she managed nothing more than a gasp for breath.

"The police are on the way," he told Marcus. "It's over. You've nowhere to go."

Veda was still on the floor, coughing and sputtering. She looked up and saw Marcus put the gun to his mouth. It all happened in the blink of an eye and yet it seemed to unfold in slow motion. Jon lunged across the attic and slammed into her uncle. The momentum sent them crashing into boxes as the report of the weapon temporarily deafened Veda.

Marcus lay on the floor facedown. The gun had fallen from his hand. Veda crawled toward the weapon, but Jon beat her to it. He put the gun to the back of her uncle's head.

"Don't do it," Veda whispered. "That's what he wants."

"Don't worry," Jon said. "He's not getting off that easy."

"How did you know where to find me?" she asked a little while later when the dust had settled and she and Jon had given their statements. Owen would be released as early as that afternoon. Her mother was finally resting. Nate, like Veda, was still processing everything.

She'd driven home from the station to shower and change

clothes. She'd spent a long time scrubbing her skin, but nothing could wash away the awful memories.

Jon put his arm around her and pulled her close. "Your mother told me where you were."

She turned. "You went to the hospital?"

"I saw Nate at the station. He told me what happened. I took the chance that she would talk to me. Something you said about the night your dad died kept bothering me. You said Lily sat stoic and tearless until your uncle tried to comfort her. Then she started screaming."

Veda shivered. "It seems so obvious, doesn't it? I don't know why I never put it together. I should have known. The signs were all there."

"You were a child when it happened. None of this is your fault. It's not your mother's fault, either. She didn't know, although she had a sense something was wrong. That was why she wanted to come back home in the middle of a storm."

"And that's why Marcus disappeared from our lives after Dad died. He was afraid Lily would say something."

"I'm sure he threatened her to keep silent. Probably told her something bad would happen to her parents if she talked. And then something bad did happen."

"That's why she blamed herself." Veda wiped a hand across her eyes. "This is all so messed up. So tragic. Two lives cut short because of him. All our lives changed forever. How do we get past it? I wouldn't blame you if you never wanted to see me again."

"Everything we've been through…the pain, the loss… it's brought us to this moment." His lips brushed her hair. "I could sit here and tell you that I never want to leave your side, which is true. At this moment, it's true. But remember what you told me about making important decisions, let alone commitments. After everything we've been through, our emotions and judgment are unreliable."

She looked up into those piercing blue eyes and managed a smile. "But if we still feel the same way in six months…"

"I'll come and find you," he said. "Wild horses couldn't keep me away."

* * * * *